Of Blood & Roses

WARRING HEARTS BOOK 1
by
GEORGIANA KENT

Copyright

---

1. https://bit.ly/keymasterchronicles

Table of Contents

Warring Hearts Saga

*~ A series of standalone steamy fantasy romance retellings with ACOTAR vibes, set in Georgiana Kent's world of Myrrithia. Adventure, *action* and HEAs guaranteed ~*

Of Blood & Roses

A *Hades and Persephone* retelling. When a human girl is forced to marry the vampire Emperor Amias de Marc, her mind is far more focused on revenge than seduction... Or so she thought... Expect forced marriage, forced proximity, stabby heroines, and swoonworthy morally grey heroes!

https://books2read.com/OfBloodAndRoses

Of Wings & Fury

Fourth Wing meets *Romeo and Juliet*. Death is not new to the students of Nathair Caisteal, the dragon rider school of Draakonia. But when Princess Idalia of the Summer Court is targeted, all eyes turn to Prince Boreas of the Winter Court. Though, despite their families' disagreements, he is not to blame. Desperate to clear his name, he agrees to help keep her alive at all costs. And falling in love is most definitely not on the agenda.

Are you prepared for the greatest forbidden romance in history? Expect forced proximity, 'he falls first', morally grey heroes, dragons and star-crossed love.

Coming December 2024
[Sign up to my Romantasy Books mailing list to be the first to see the cover and be notified of pre-orders and ARC opportunities:
https://beacons.ai/georgianakentbooks]

Of Airs & Vanity

A *Pride and Prejudice* retelling. When the aloof Unicorn Lord, Vasilis of Izan, visits his friend in the little town of Eldermoor, he expects nothing more than the usual dinner parties and marriage-hungry mothers. But when his friend is wrongly arrested, he joins forces with the sister of his friend's fiancée, the formidable Elyssia Bracemell, to help clear his name. Can they work together without gauging out the other's eyes or, even worse, falling in love?
Grumpy-sunshine meets the ultimate enemy to lovers chaos!
Pre-order coming soon!
[This novel will be free to subscribers. Sign up to my Romantasy Books mailing list to be the first to see its cover and receive it for free
https://beacons.ai/georgianakentbooks]

URBAN FANTASY
ROMANCE

~ A series of urban fantasy romances sharing the same universe with Georgiana's unique blend of East Asian myths, shifters, Time travel, mystery and slow burn romantic tension ~

Soul Dominion (1 – 3)
Erica's Story

Keys of Time
https://books2read.com/KeysofTime
Keys of Fate
https://books2read.com/KeysofFate
Keys of Death
https://books2read.com/KeysofDeath

Soul Dominion (4 - 6)
Nathaniel's Story

Coming soon!
*[Sign up to my Soul Dominion mailing list to be the first to see covers and be notified of pre-orders and ARC opportunities: **https://beacons.ai/ georgianakentbooks**]*

Prequel Novellas

KeyMaster Origins
https://books.georgianakent.com/KeyMasterOrigins

Dedications

To All Who Love Morally Grey Heroes With Fangs Who Talk Dirty
and Fuck Hard

Triggers

References to terminal illness, family grief, and off-screen infant mortality. All romance is consensual and hot. So damn hot.

Of Blood & Roses

Perfect for fans of *A Court of Thorns and Roses*, this fantasy romance retelling of *Hades and Persephone* about a human girl and her forced marriage to the cold yet striking King of the Undead is impossible to put down!

In exchange for protection, the Night Lord and King of Forever has two requests of the people of Noxterra: a willing supply of blood victims and a wife.

Every hundred years, the vampire Emperor Amias de Marc opens the gates to his Eternal Palace to select a human bride. In 'The Picking', unmarried maidens turning twenty in the winter are requested to attend and, from them, the one to make the flowers bloom becomes his betrothed. Refusal means certain death.

Lamia Fontaine is a girl hell-bent on revenge. And her target is the Emperor. Lucky for her, she's part of The Picking and has an invitation to attend the palace. Now, all she needs is to get close enough to strike...

*Of Blood & Roses is a complete *standalone, enemies-to-lovers novel* inspired by Hades and Persephone. With magic, spice and a guaranteed happily ever after—it's perfect for fantasy romance fans looking for their next hot, ship-worthy couple!*

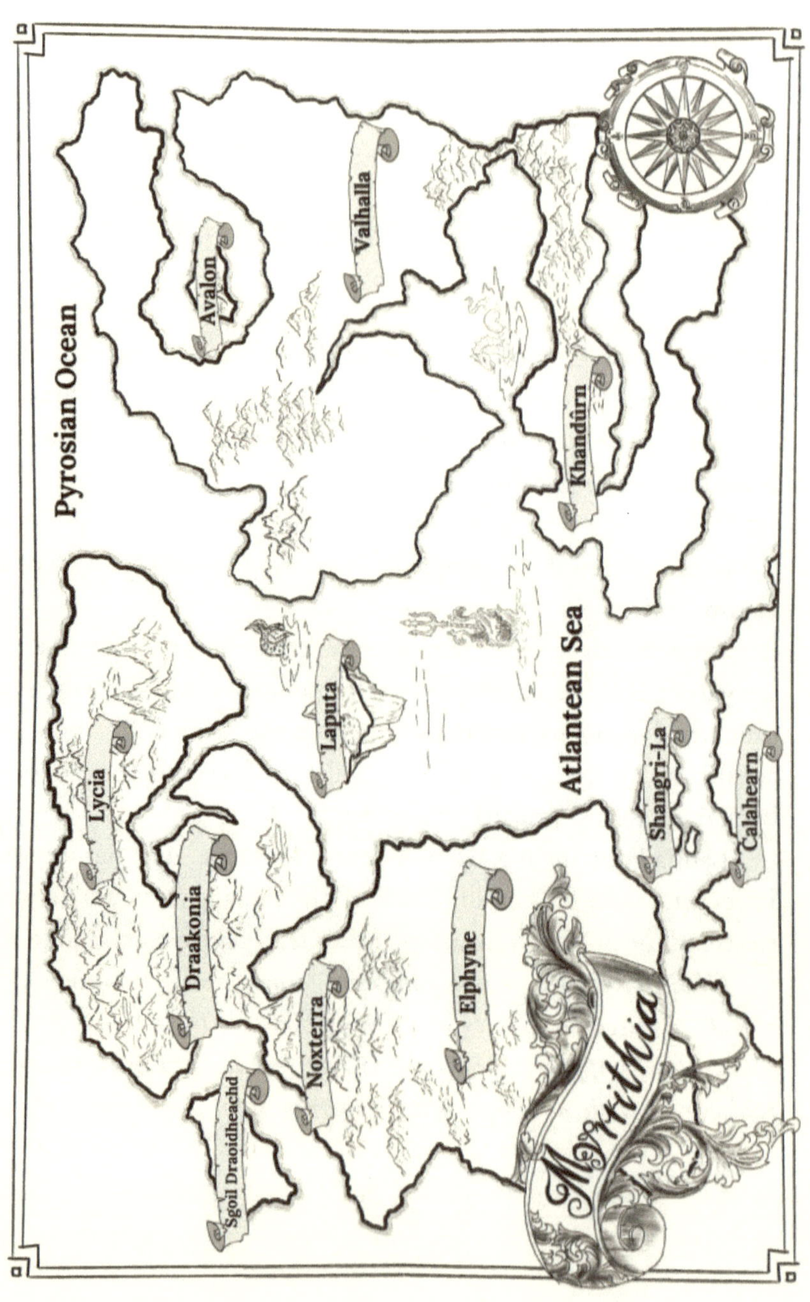
Pyrosian Ocean
Avalon
Valhalla
Khandûrn
Atlantean Sea
Lycia
Laputa
Shangri-La
Calahearn
Draakonia
Noxterra
Elphyne
Sgoil Draoidheachd
Morrithia

Prologue

***

In exchange for protection, Emperor Amias de Marc, King of Forever, Lord of the Night, and self-proclaimed God of Death, has two requests of the people of Noxterra: a willing supply of Blood Sacrifices and a wife.

The selection for becoming a Blood Sacrifice is civil and the right of every citizen of Noxterra. Only the old and infirm who do not wish to pass away naturally, or let their illness ravage them, may apply. The application process is rigid to avoid exploitation. To be selected is an honour and celebrated by the families of Blood Sacrifices.

The selection of a bride for the King of Forever is less so.

Once every hundred years, a bride is selected for Emperor Amias in a ceremony known as 'The Picking'. All unmarried maidens turning twenty in the winter of The Picking receive a royal invitation to attend the Eternal Palace. From them, the one to make the flowers bloom shall become his betrothed.

To be chosen is both a privilege and a curse. Refusal means certain death.

1

One Day

900 years previous

Amias trailed his fingers along the upper arm of one of his bedmates: silky smooth and porcelain white under his touch. The maiden sighed in her sleep, her long black hair covering her like a blanket. Settling against the cushions, he folded his arms behind his head as his second bedmate snuggled up against him with a sleepy murmur. The odd puncture mark marred the skin around their breasts, blood smearing their curves. Thankfully, Madame Ostara had come to accept his blood play when in the heat of passion and would not worry about the damage it made. In any case, he paid handsomely for the pleasure.

He preferred it this way: sex was sex. After his wife had passed away almost a hundred years ago, he had vowed never to love again, unwilling to revisit such grief. He still felt her loss keenly and doubted he would ever find love again, especially as she had known him before his change to a vampire. She had known him as the Fæ he was before he had been bitten whilst saving their child from a Strigoi and hadn't seen him as the monster he was now. Infected and transformed by the Strigoi, he could never find another so understanding, for who could love an abomination as cold and as bloodthirsty as he?

Though he had paid for their company until the morn, sleep eluded him, as it often had these hundred years. One of the few disadvantages of being a vampire. Though, the perks were certainly not to be sniffed at: invulnerability, immortality and super strength. Not only had they helped him establish rule over Elphyne—coming to the aid of the Winter and Summer Courts of Elphyne to vanquish marauding orcs—but they had allowed him to come to the aid of Noxterra, the mountainous country neighbouring his own.

Two years previously, the Chimera of Lycia, West Myrrithia's northernmost country, had invaded Noxterra. The Chimera were deadly. A fire-breathing hybrid that humans stood no chance against, and which left nothing but death and destruction in their wake. When King Neclik and his army had perished in the first battle, the people of Noxterra had cried out for help.

And so, he had answered.

Leaving his oldest son in charge, he had gathered his army and left for Noxterra. For the sake of the Noxterrans, but also for the sake of Elphyne and its people. To avoid any possible invasion of his own kingdom and home.

It had not been easy, though, despite his vampiric power. The fighting had been long and brutal, and he had lost many, many good men. But, just yesterday, in an almighty battle outside the capital city of Dårath, he had been victorious in slaughtering the Chimeran ruler, Merikh. The remaining Chimera had turned tail, fleeing back to Lycia. Proclaimed a hero, national celebrations were announced and parties and revelry replaced bloodshed and fear.

But he was ready to go home. Despite the pleasure of the last few hours, it wasn't enough to fill the void inside. He was restless. He put it down to missing the forests of Elphyne. Though he had been turned into a vampire, his Fæ instincts remained strong and he longed for the ancient trees of his homeland, the whisper of their leaves upon the breeze, and the smell of rain on their grassy banks. The bleak rocky crags of the Noxterran mountains jarred whatever soul remained within him. Even the soil here felt different between his fingers!

Extricating his naked body from those of Madame Ostara's finest girls, Amias hunted for his garments. Once dressed, he quietly left the bedchamber, finding Altair, Badar and Ciro, his three Felidaeon, standing guard. These large, over-sized cats were native to the mountains of Noxterra, navigating their sheer slopes with sure-footed ease. Discovering these three as orphaned cubs when on patrol soon after his arrival, Amias had taken them in, nurturing them back to strength. Choosing to remain with him, rather than return to the wild, they had proved invaluable in skirmishes. Not to mention excellent companions on lonely days.

With the three Felidaeon by his side, he swept out of the parlour and onto the lively streets of Dårath. Enchanted torches lit up the stall-lined streets, selling drink and food and pleasure to punters eager to celebrate their survival and freedom. The towering palace of the former king reached heavenwards to the glowing twin moons of Myrrithia. Though he and his court had been permitted use of the palace, he disliked its dark stone and longed for his treetop palace in Elphyne. Unease immediately set in as memories of the day's meeting tumbled through his mind. He continued past Palace Way, the swooping bridge that led to the palace's entrance, turning his feet to the palace gardens and the woodland within. He would rest there tonight, he decided.

Picking his way through the forest with the help of the moon's glow and his own keen eyes, he walked deep into the green heart of the woodland. The trees here weren't as ancient as those in Elphyne and the creeks of their boughs were less sonorous, but the rustle of their leaves still soothed him, succeeding in banishing the sense of foreboding that had settled on him since the meeting: the remaining barons of Noxterra had gathered in Dårath to meet with him, requesting he stayed indefinitely as ruler to protect them from the

Chimera, alongside his responsibilities in Elphyne. Though he feared for the Noxterrans, Amias had no desire to begin an empire.

The trees thinned, and a clearing opened before him. Walking through the ferns and wildflowers, he came to a quaint thatched cottage. It looked deserted, but he avoided it, continuing his way through the forest. Not long after, his Felidaeon raised their hackles, slowing their pace as growls rumbled deep within. Slowing also, he caught the distant sound of arguments and scuffling, like a struggle. Sadly, bandits had taken advantage of the disarray and marauding had become rife. Another thing he had to resolve before leaving for home.

He was on the edge of the forest now. Unsheathing his sword in preparation, he crept through the last few trees, careful to avoid twigs and anything else that might give away his presence. He found himself at the brow of a dale. Lying flat behind a swath of gorse bushes, the Felidaeon crouching nearby; he inhaled sharply.

By the gods, surely not?!

There, down in the valley, by the shores of a lake, was a tree with glowing pink flowers.

An Elixium tree!

He'd heard legends of them and their healing powers, but never, not in all his long years, had he seen one! The very earth seemed to hum with its divinity. Though it looked worse for wear, with broken branches and patches of foliage missing.

The sound of more scuffling drew him from his reverie, and he noticed a couple grappling with one another. A lifeless body lay sprawled across the tangle of roots, its hand clutching at a loose branch of the tree.

Were they fighting over it?!

They would destroy it!

Without thinking, he rose from his hiding place and advanced down the valley, leaping on to Altair's back. With the other two cats flanking him, he charged them. But the men were too engrossed in their fighting to pay him any heed until it was too late. Ciro and Badar pounced to knock them to the ground. Dismounting, Amias pointed his sword at the two men.

"Explain yourself!"

"King Amias!" one man cried, cowering behind his arms as the other flinched away from the Felidaeon's snapping jaws.

"Ciro! Heel!"

The Felidaeon snarled, canines bared, but pulled back to prowl the perimeter.

"Explain yourself!" Amias repeated to the men, jabbing his blade into their sternums. "What happened here?"

The men looked sheepish and remained quiet.

His nostrils flared to smell the dead man's blood. Amias glanced from the branch with its magical blossom to the dead body, its spilled blood tarnishing the roots red, and back again. Inspiration struck. His mind was made up. "My patience wears thin," he said through gritted teeth, fangs flashing. "I said 'explain yourself'. This is my land. You are trespassing."

"Your land? You're staying?" One man stammered, looking guilty. "Forgive us! We didn't realise."

"This woodland is now mine. Be gone. Or you will pay the price for this man's death."

"It was an accident!"

"He slipped!"

"Be that as it may, but continue to plunder the trees on my land and you will answer to me. Do you understand?" His eyes blazed crimson.

The men stared at him in shock.

The three Felidaeon roared, and they flinched, whimpering in fear. "We understand! Sorry, Your Excellency!"

Scrambling to their feet, they cast a backwards glance at the branch with its pink flowers, caught the fearsome gaze of Amias and his Felidaeon and fled back up the dale.

Amias looked up into the glowing crown of the Elixium tree. Reaching out a shaking hand, he pressed it against the trunk, almost feeling the magic and power coursing through its wood and boughs.

He bowed his head in reverence. "You are safe now."

Dragging the body away, he noted the discolouration on the bark where the man's blood had soaked the roots. It webbed up the side of the tree like some dark evil. When he touched it, he immediately withdrew his hand, disliking the sense of deadness beneath their fingertips. Fetching out a small, iridescent stone, he breathed on it, igniting it. It flashed hot-white.

"Yes, Your Majesty? Is everything alright?" A tinny voice arose from the stone's centre.

"I'm taking Noxterra. All of it. Every tree and stone. Assemble the Barons in the Central Court to discuss my conditions within the hour. Kill all who resist. And bring a unit of men to the palace's woodlands. There's something I wish them to guard for me."

Returning the stone to his pocket, he leaned back, looking up through the pink petals at the starry sky above. It wasn't home, but it would be.

One day.

2

The Picking

Present day

The people of Noxterra have lived happily under the rule of Emperor Amias de Marc, Night Lord and King of Forever, for almost a millennium. On the whole, Emperor Amias was a fair ruler and the mountain kingdom of Noxterra had flourished to become one of Myrrithia's greatest. Provided Blood Sacrifices and a bride were given.

Whilst selection for a bride only took place once every hundred years, with so many potential brides, The Picking lasted a week. For this reason, Emperor Amias granted it as a public holiday to the people of Noxterra. Towns and cities celebrated with markets, festivals, and merriment. However, as the capital and host city of The Picking, the people of Dårath liked to put on the biggest and greatest show. Though it was bittersweet. Because, as people celebrated, they were keenly aware of the chosen bride's sacrifice as the vampire emperor's consort.

BLESSED WITH OUTCROPS of land that provided shelter from the waves and wind, Gerran had grown to be one of Noxterra's largest coastal cities. With one of the best natural harbours this side of the Atlantean Sea, trade had naturally come, and with it, jobs.

The Fontaines had moved to Gerran several generations past, establishing a profitable accountancy business for the merchants who traded there. Though, whilst it helped them escape poverty, it didn't mean all hardships escaped them...

It was early spring and the day invitations to The Picking were to be delivered. With it being such a rare event, the Baron of Gerran had organised a festival for the town's folk. Alongside food stalls and games, a stage had been erected in the town square next to the statue of 'The Barons', a statue to commemorate the hundreds who had died when they tried to revolt against Emperor Amias' extreme demands on becoming ruler of Noxterra. They had forfeited their lives.

The stage was festooned with flowers and brightly coloured streamers. As midday approached, the Baron stepped on to the stage and an eerie quiet settled upon the gathered crowds. In his hand, he held several envelopes bearing the black seal of the Night Lord.

It was unnecessary, though. The girls knew who they were, as did most of the town. Whilst most parents had attempted to find suitors for their daughters before today, some had slipped through, either through personal determination to attend The Picking, or through no fault of their own.

As their names were read out, they mounted the stage, accepting their invitation to attend the Eternal Palace before lining up behind the Baron.

"Lamia Fontaine!"

A tall girl with silky brown skin stepped forward, her expression determined as she took the envelope from the Baron with a curtsy. Lining up with the other three girls, a grim satisfaction settled upon her, despite the shadows under her eyes. Though her parents had found many suitors to help avoid this, she had refused every single one. Her mind was too overcome by grief to think of marriage, she had said.

But she was finally where she wanted to be. She was that step closer to getting her revenge on the man who ruined her life.

And it would taste so, so sweet.

TWO MONTHS LATER MARKED the start of The Picking. A week-long event with those maidens turning twenty in the winter arriving in the capital from all over the kingdom. Carriages and horses filled the mountain roads leading to the capital city of Dårath, which was nestled amidst Noxterra's mightiest peaks.

There was much celebration made of the arrival of potential brides who wore the finest white gowns their families could afford. Bands played music and rice and petals were thrown like confetti. Swathes of red and white roses decorated Dårath Boulevard, the main road that led to the black and gold gates of the Eternal Palace. It was along this road that the brides sat in fine open-topped carriages pulled by Felidaeon, large Noxterran black cats with smooth fur and tufts of hair on the tips of their ears.

With Noxterra being so far north, there was little sunlight, even as summer approached, and the wind carried a constant chill. Nonetheless, the people of Dårath greeted the brides warmly as they paraded down the main boulevard, setting off magic firelights, playing music and waving and cheering their procession onto Palace Way: an elevated bridge lined with towers that passed over the canals of Dårath. However, whilst the city continued their celebrations with drink and revelry, the brides and their families reported to the Hall of the Brides, located at the end of the bridge and next door to the black Eternal Palace, where Emperor Amias resided.

As the doors to the Hall were shut, muffling the cheers of the city, the reality of their situation hit most brides who would either break down in tears or collapse, having to be revived with smelling salts by the Emperor's attendants.

But not Lamia Fontaine.

Like all brides, Lamia had been allocated a day for The Picking. Arriving as requested, she could hardly remember her procession through Dårath with her mother and father. Dressed in a becoming off-the shoulder gown with airy skirts and glittery lace, all she could remember through the noise and chaos was the feel of the cold blade hidden in her garter.

As with all Noxterrans, Lamia's hair was as black as raven feathers. Though, unlike pure-blooded Noxterrans, hers was curly and her skin a lustrous brown, a sign of her heritage from Khandûrn, a country east across the Atlantean Sea. Normally she left it untamed, but today she'd gone to great lengths to create an attractive chignon, pinned in place with a diamond slide.

"Isn't this spectacular, darling?" her mother cried as her wide eyes took in the golden cornices and friezes of the Hall of the Brides.

Her mother was native Noxterran with dark hair, dazzling blue eyes, and pale skin. Though, at this precise moment, a touch of colour brightened her cheeks.

Lamia cut her mother a derisive look, the blue eyes she'd inherited from her gleaming coolly. Delilah Fontaine had always had a soft spot for anything shiny. Though her daughter was facing possible forced marriage to the most powerful Fæ in the land, and a vampire no less, the gold gilt decorations met with her approval.

It had been the same when she'd hosted her brother's farewell party.

Miklaus Fontaine patted his wife on the shoulder, smiling indulgently at her, before tucking a stray curl behind Lamia's ear. "Yes, dear, and Lamia is almost as spectacular."

He gave Lamia a wink, and she covered her smile with a gloved hand.

Miklaus Fontaine was an accountant from Gerran, situated on the coast. Though not the most exciting of trades, it paid well and had allowed him to give his family everything they needed, and more. It was his side of the family who were Khandûrni and Lamia had inherited her dark skin and curly hair from him.

They were sat waiting for Lamia's name to be read out. The Hall was busy with families preparing brides for the task that lay ahead. Which was difficult, as no one knew exactly what that was, for little was known of the process for The Picking.

Lamia cast a critical eye over the friezes depicting chasteness, deference and love. The ideal qualities of a future consort for the Forever King.

She just needed to get close enough...

"He killed all the children of Dårath when he first came to power."

Lamia turned at the sound of the hushed voices to find a small cluster of potential brides huddled together.

"Didn't he drain their blood and bathe in it?"

"That's what the legends say. I heard he'll drink the blood of any bride who refuses to do *exactly* what he wants."

She bit her lip as if the thought was thrilling beyond words.

"They say he's over a thousand years old, but hung like a wolfman!"

Lamia scoffed silently to herself, ignoring their peel of giggles. Little was known about the Emperor. Some legends say he came to the aid of Noxterra and was asked to stay. Some said he settled here because of its dark skies and short days. In any case, he rarely left his kingdom. Instead, he relied on his appointed Barons to manage his cities. Any whiff of rebellion was quickly quashed by his elite and most feared battalion: the Knights of Eternal Darkness. Not that the people spoke of rebellion. Despite his vampiric nature, the Emperor of Forever was respected by Noxterra, for without him and his Knights, the beasts of Lycia would be upon them once more.

"I found him quite congenial when he heard our case in the Central Court. Cold, but fair. And clever. Don't believe everything you hear. People change, especially one so old," said her father, leaning close, his eyes on the brides.

Lamia looked over at him. He'd mentioned his visit to the Eternal Palace many times over the years. Before, it had just seemed like some distant, dreamlike place, but not now. Now it seemed frighteningly real.

The double doors at the far end of the Hall opened, and a Herald emerged dressed in the red and black livery of the Forever King.

"Coraline Elder!"

There was an audible wail as the bride in question gaped in horror at the sound of her name being called. A hush befell the Hall as all eyes turned to her. It was almost lunchtime on the fourth day of The Picking. Would she be the long-awaited bride?

After a stunned moment, her parents, tears in their eyes, guided Coraline to her feet to embrace her. With a last look, she stumbled to the door and was ushered through.

The doors closed behind her, and an uneasy silence befell the Hall.

"We will await you outside," Lamia's father said in a low voice as he watched a palace attendant comfort Coraline's parents. Sniffling into a handkerchief, the mother let herself be guided out of the door with her husband to the black and gold gates of the Eternal Palace, where unsuccessful brides were returned.

Where they had last seen her brother...

"And," he continued, "if you are successful, my darling, I'm sure we shall be permitted to see you within the next couple of days."

Lamia nodded numbly as her father took her hand and squeezed it reassuringly.

"He is said to be very handsome and, erh, his reputation precedes him." Her mother blushed, filling the silence. "Do your duty and you might just like it."

"Delilah!" her father gasped.

"Well, I did," she smiled coyly at him.

It was his turn to blush.

He cleared his throat, turning his attention back to Lamia, who was looking at the ground as if willing it to swallow her whole. "You shall be fine."

Surprised, Lamia found her father's hands appear over hers, which were gripping the lace of her skirts, their knuckles white.

Laughing nervously, Lamia unclenched her fists, smoothing her skirts to avoid attention being drawn to the blade hidden within. "Of course, father."

She looked away, not wanting him to see the hollow truth there. She had no intention of returning.

As time ticked by and the afternoon sun swung low, Lamia began to wonder if Coraline had been successful. The Herald was certainly taking longer to return to the Hall than on previous occasions. Maybe she had made the flowers bloom and was now wife to the Emperor? Maybe Lamia had lost her one chance to kill the bastard vampire and get her revenge on the thing that had ruined her life?

Surely the gods couldn't be so cruel?! Would they not give her the revenge she so desired?

Then the double doors opened once more to reveal the Herald.

Lamia felt the bitterness in her stomach subside.

Good, Coraline had been unsuccessful.

"Lamia Fontaine!"

Taking a deep breath, Lamia was vaguely aware of her mother's anxiety as all three of them stood together. Letting her parents embrace her, she made sure she told them she loved them before returning their embrace. After all, this would be the last time they saw her alive. She doubted she'd be able to escape once she'd killed the Emperor.

Then, half-listening to their promises to see her soon, she walked forward to the Herald.

3

The Flowers that Bloom

Flinching as the door shut behind her, Lamia stood for a moment, rooted to the spot.

"This way, please, Miss Fontaine," the Herald said, walking down a mirrored gallery.

The mirrors had been polished until they shone like diamonds, reflecting them back a thousand-fold. The repeated images made her giddy, and she turned her attention to the anger within, which had been her constant companion since last year, letting her mind wander to the Emperor and the destruction she would exact.

Lamia glanced at the Herald as he led her towards a set of doors. He was Noxterran, with raven dark hair and blue eyes. Definitely human and not some blood-sucker. She'd always wondered how much of the Emperor's staff was human. It made sense since the Emperor was restricted when he could leave the palace, but still...

How could they? How could they serve such a beast?

Exiting the doors, Lamia found herself stepping back on to the grand bridge of Palace Way. The peaks surrounding the city were a pale lilac in the late afternoon light. Even at this time of year, their sides were peppered with snowfall. The Eternal Palace rose on her right, its dark tower splintering the heavens above. The palace was acclaimed for the mighty circular stained-glass that dominated the front façade.

An unearthly glow emanated from it, casting brilliant shards of colour upon the stone of the bridge and the waters below.

Some people referred to the palace as the Black Palace, not only because its Emperor was a Child of the Night but also because of the black stone it was built from, smooth and shimmering, like fragments of the night sky itself. Its famed black battlements and turrets towered high above her. Sturdy flying buttresses protruded like spider legs and she could spy a large, vaulted apse on the left with blood-red roof tiles. This was said to be the State Chapel and where the Emperor wed his bride.

She shuddered involuntarily.

Beyond that was a wing with tall windows and bright blue roof tiles with skylights just visible. And then, beside it, a wing made entirely of glass...

"Are you cold, Miss Fontaine?" The Herald asked as he guided her towards the entrance within the colossal stained-glass window.

The sun was setting, scorching the rooftops and waters of Dårath's canals with its pinks and yellows and oranges. It glinted off the Eternal Palace, igniting the black stone of its walls to reveal marbled bands of purple and blue. Veins of gold threaded through it like fine silk. It was breathtaking. The view was so beautiful it made her heart ache.

"No, I'm well, thank you," she replied, pushing her shoulders back, refusing to give in to sentiment. The gods must be smiling on her, granting her such a glorious last sunset.

Those on duty saluted her arrival: the Knights of Eternal Darkness. The Emperor's elite guards. They were dressed in full black body armour and chain mail. Plumes of the deepest red topped their decorative helmets.

Passing through the entrance, she came to a sudden standstill.

She found herself in a grand entranceway. A large butterfly staircase in black marble veined in gold led high into the tower, whilst an extravagant black crystal chandelier drooped low, its iridescent sparkles mixing with the reflections from the window to scatter like broken rainbows, igniting the sombre interior. She'd been nowhere as exquisite as this!

Noticing tittering, she looked to see a small group of women dressed in fine gowns, their hair piled high upon their heads. Glistening jewels adorned their necks. They were eyeing her with curiosity, hiding smiles and giggles behind their hands. Though, one woman with blonde hair stood watching her, her blue eyes steady and unreadable. Her ears were pointed like a Fæ.

"Please follow me, Miss Fontaine."

And the Herald led her down a corridor on the left. Constructed from the same black marble, the only illumination was from the enchanted torches. Their polychromatic glow reflected off the polished floor. This corridor was decorated with curios from the far corners of Myrrithia: chinaware from Shangri-la, shells from Atlantis, and silver feathers from Laputa. She'd spent all her life in Noxterra and had never seen such wonders. A pang of sorrow cut her deep as she realised she would never get the chance to see them now.

Head held high, she continued down the corridor. The *clip-clip* of her heels echoed on the tiled floor and she began to wonder how much further they had to go.

"Not long now, Miss Fontaine." The Herald said, as if reading her mind.

Sure enough, the next set of double doors was flanked by two guards. The Herald opened them to reveal a grand chapel made of black marble and lit from the same enchanted torches. And Felidaeon. Three of them, their amber cat-eyes glowing through the gloom. They each wore a chain of gold around their necks.

She felt as if her insides had turned to stone.

He had Felidaeon! Could she still do this?! She set her shoulders back, trying to banish the icy fear threatening to take over. *Well, if she were to be mauled to death, it would be worth it if she took him with her...*

"Time is running out!" snapped a vexed voice.

"Patience, Your Excellency."

"I ran out of that a long time ago," the voice growled. "It's not as if I am demanding a love match, just a wife."

"I understand, Your Excellency. But it must be the *right* wife. The flowers know. The Picking has never failed you."

Lamia nervously dragged her eyes from the Felidaeon to find a High Priest waiting on an opulent seat made of ebony and lined with red velvet. And, before the altar, where a bouquet of dead roses rested, paced the King of Forever. Emperor Amias de Marc himself.

"Miss Lamia Fontaine of Garren, Your Excellency."

The Emperor whirled round at the announcement, the cold scowl and clenched jaw immediately softening to surprise on seeing her.

Having announced her, the Herald stood to the side to permit her entrance.

Keeping one wary eye on the Felidaeon, Lamia advanced in the slow sashaying walk she'd practised time and time again with her mother.

Despite herself, she inhaled at the Emperor's cold beauty. She had never seen him before. Portraits of him were rare, but his vampiric charm, and that of his offspring, was legendary across the whole of Noxterra. He looked in his mid- to late thirties, though, if rumours were true, he was closer to 1100 years.

He had his long black hair tied back, revealing pointed ears, inhumanly pale skin, sensual lips, and a cold violet gaze. He was wearing a black cape adorned with a lavish collar of black raven feathers over a smartly fitted jerkin and breeches that emphasised his physique. A simple iron crown with a red gem adorned his head: his Imperial Crown. He was terrible and beautiful all at once.

Coming to a stop, he appraised her with interest, taking in her exposed neck, collarbone, and smooth shoulders. The glittering lace of her gown hinted at the flesh and curves hidden below, whilst the slit in her skirts teased. She'd purposely chosen a more risqué dress in the hope that it would divert his attention from her blade.

It was working.

Catching his gaze, she plunged into a deep curtesy, like those her mother had made her practice, but lower. The better for showing off her natural assets. "Your Excellency."

There was a moment of quiet before he spoke. "Arise, Miss Fontaine."

His voice was deep and honey-smooth and seemed to luxuriate in the sound of her name, sending shivers coursing through her.

When she stood once more, she found him walking over to her, circling her with an appreciative air. Not unsimilar to a Felidaeon circling potential food. Her gaze flitted nervously to the three big cats seated nearby, their tails twitching. Clasping her hands together, she forced herself to breathe slowly, to calm her nerves.

Not yet... He wasn't close enough...

"You are Khandûrni?" he asked, violet eyes roaming over her like a connoisseur.

Taken aback, she glanced over at the Herald, who gave her a small smile of encouragement.

"Yes, Your Excellency. On my father's side."

"I see. You are enchanting."

Her eyes glanced up in surprise, her insides churning in anxious knots. "Thank you, Your Excellency."

He inhaled sharply as her blue irises met his purple. "Your mother is Noxterran? You have her eyes... How striking!"

The Emperor turned to nod at the High Priest, who rose and came towards her, gesturing her to kneel upon a red cushion on the tiled floor.

She knelt, head bowed and heart pounding as he made the sign of a circle.

"We ask the Gods of Old to bless this Picking of a bride. *Varikaii o Pactos.*"

"*Varikaii o Pactos.*" Intoned the Emperor and Herald. Lamia followed suit.

"You understand, my child, that if you succeed in making the roses bloom, you are automatically proclaimed wife of Emperor Amias de Marc and Queen of Noxterra?"

Her heart stilled, and it was then that Lamia felt the gravity of the situation. So fixated had she been on her pursuit of vengeance she had given little thought to the possibility of becoming this monster's wife...

"I... I understand," she stammered.

A hand was offered to her, and she looked up in surprise to find it the Emperor's. Shyly, she placed her hand in his and shivered at its coolness.

Helping her to her feet, Emperor Amias stepped to the side, bowing and gesturing for her to approach the altar. Bowing reverently before the altar to the gods, she lifted her skirts and ascended the steps leading to the altar with the rotten bouquet upon it. Its marred leaves and brown petals made for a sorry sight. A gleaming, clean knife lay next to it upon a red cloth.

She licked her lips at the sight of the blade.

"As you know, Miss Fontaine, my bride is the one who makes the flowers bloom. A tradition that has served me well for a millennium," the Emperor said, voice low.

It thrummed through her and, though he was behind her and she had only just met him, she could see him before her in perfect detail. She swallowed down the fluttering in her stomach.

"To do that, you must allow a drop of your blood to land on the roses you see before you. For it is the life-force in my Queen's blood that I need to sire children. Everything else is a *bonus.*"

Lamia shook off the unsettling vibrations of his voice and reached for the blade. "Just a drop, Your Excellency?"

"Aye, just a drop."

She could feel the King of Forever take a step closer.

That's it, you devil. Come closer…

She set the blade against her left palm and heard him come closer still, like a moth to a flame.

Stealing herself against the sharp edge, she sliced down, and crimson bloomed.

The metallic smell of her blood hit her and there was a sharp inhale behind her.

"Quickly!" The Emperor hissed.

Holding her clasped hand aloft with a wince, she let the red ooze and trickle, dripping onto the decayed flowers.

The chapel was deathly quiet as the Emperor, Priest and Herald watched the bouquet and waited.

She could feel his body just behind her now, drawn to her and the smell of blood as only a vampire could. Anticipation crackled in the chapel and, with everyone's attention so diverted, she spun round and plunged the knife down.

With a roar, the three Felidaeon attacked as the Priest and Herald ran to their king's aid. But Emperor Amias stood his ground, catching the blade calmly between his two palms. He called the beasts off, which chose to prowl nearby instead, hackles raised, eyes blazing and teeth bared.

Violet eyes caught her blue, his look of fury melting away to mirth as she tried to wrench the blade free, tried to plunge it through his cruel heart, but couldn't. It was like the blade was wedged between two mountains and not merely between two palms. But it had been so easy in her dreams! She had succeeded…

"NO!"

Crying out like a wild beast as she failed to prise the blade away, she changed her stance and tried again and again, tugging with all her might, but to no avail. It was stuck fast.

The nearest Felidaeon growled, and she looked over at it warily, gasping from the exertion. At first, she didn't notice the cries of joy from the High Priest or those of disbelief from the Herald.

Alerted, Emperor Amias moved his attention away from his would-be assailant and to the roses that had been dead.

They shimmered and glowed, flaring with magic that burned the decay away. Redness bloomed, smoothing away the brown rot and decay from the petals. Sweeping down and along to colour the woody stems and thorns and leaves and blooms of the other flowers. Within seconds, a lush bouquet of fresh roses rested upon the altar.

The High Priest began chanting, making the circle of blessing before the Emperor and Lamia, her hands still wrapped round the hilt of the dagger.

"The flowers bloom! All hail the Queen!" came the combined voices of the High Priest and the Herald as they bowed before her.

Emperor Amias smiled down at her, fangs gleaming. "Well met, Wife."

4

Knife's Edge

"**N**O!" she cried, battering her free fist against the Emperor's chest.

In one quick movement, the Emperor knocked the knife out of her hands, sending it skittering across the floor of the chapel. He then took both her hands in his steely grip, wrenching her closer.

"Oh yes, My Queen. The Gods do not lie. Your blood brought the flower to life. You are destined for me."

Destined...

The thought made her want to scream and kiss him all at once.

Stunned at the raging emotions within, she stopped fighting and breathlessly watched him take the bouquet off the altar. Letting go of her hands, he presented it to her with a slight bow.

"For you, My Queen."

In a blaze of fury, she swiped the flowers from his hand, scattering them upon the floor where the Felidaeon sniffed them with curiosity.

A momentary flicker of surprise was followed by a glimpse of hurt before a sultry look banished it away.

He leaned forward, eyes burning. "Feisty. I hope this foretells of *other* delights."

Lamia coloured before remembering her anger. "Never! I'll never give myself to a monster like you!" she snarled. "To a murderer..."

The look of surprise appeared once more before being hidden behind a mocking stare. "I do enjoy a challenge. Shall we?"

She looked at him blankly as he offered her his arm.

With a shake of her head, she turned on her heel and descended the altar steps, crossing the Chapel to the exit. The Herald gaped at her in astonishment as she stormed passed.

SHE WALKED BLINDLY, red colouring her vision as she thundered down corridor after corridor. Doors were opened for her by surprised servants, guiding her into the heart of the palace. The distant sound of bells sounding throughout the streets of Dårath awoke her from her rage and she found herself in a corridor with one side made of glass windows that gave out over the canals. The twin moons of Myrrithia were just peeking over the horizon.

Reaching for an ornate clock upon a table, she rushed towards the glass, throwing the item at it with all her might. Bouncing off, the clock smashed to pieces on the marble floor. Momentarily startled, she was about to kneel to pick up the pieces when she heard footfall. Looking up, she saw the Emperor standing in the doorway, taking in the scene before him, flanked by his three Felidaeon, their tails flicking. He glanced at the window and stroked the Felidaeon beside him, scratching behind its ear.

"It is enchanted. All windows of the palace are. For protection. I was disliked when I first came to power..."

"I wonder why!" she snarled. "Maybe if you hadn't barged in and made demands!" She left the pieces to hurry down the corridor.

"I had my reasons," he said, flashing her a cool look.

"As all despots do!" she cried, reaching the doors. She thumped her hands against them, shooting a steely look at the servants on guard.

The servants glanced over at the Emperor for permission. He must have granted it, for the doors opened and she found herself in a ballroom. The immense hall was lit by an enchanted chandelier that drooped over the dance floor, whilst smaller enchanted torches lit up the walls and viewing gallery. Glorious arrangements of white blooms were in every corner. Everything sparkled and shone and, if she weren't trying to escape, she'd have taken a turn to admire their splendour.

Noticing several doors, she veered off to the right and ran down another corridor. If only she could find the main entranceway! Maybe she could escape and find her parents.

After several minutes of running along corridors, she found herself admitted to a room with a long dining table set out for a banquet. Fifty or so curious faces turned at her entrance. At the head of the table sat Emperor Amias, a gold goblet in his hand, the Felidaeon at his feet. Amongst the faces, Lamia recognised the woman with blonde hair from the entranceway—she was regarding her with interest.

"What a surprise to see you again, My Queen," the Emperor said drily from where he sat, legs crossed, an amused look in his eyes.

With a cry of exasperation, she turned and ran out of a different door, only to find the corridor she'd chosen led her back to the dining room within minutes. She stood in the doorway, head reeling, tears of frustration scalding her eyes.

"Why don't you sit and rest yourself? Food is waiting."

He gestured to the seat on his left. Hesitating, Lamia eyed it longingly. Her feet ached after running so much in her heels and her throat was parched. As much as she wanted to run, she needed to gather her thoughts and come up with another strategy lest she look too much like a fool.

Reluctantly, she went over to the seat, walking cautiously passed the Felidaeon—one of which nipped at her ankles—and allowed a servant to help tuck her and her skirts in.

The Emperor waved a hand and a dozen servants burst into the dining room, serving them plates of roast beef and seasonal vegetables before attending to the court. Several servants circled the table, offering them red wine or water. A separate decanter was removed from a tray of ice and its contents poured into the goblet in the Emperor's hand. Lamia was puzzled to see that the servants had presented him with a plate of beef as well.

The Emperor stood, and silence befell the Dining Room. "To our new Queen!" He raised his goblet in Lamia's direction. "To us."

Lamia scowled but rose her cup in reply. "To your demise."

There were gasps from the courtiers, but Lamia refused to look in their direction.

The Emperor smiled, inclining his head. "*Touché*, Miss Fontaine."

Sitting, he cut his beef into slithers and fed the Felidaeon in turn, which took it from him with surprising delicacy. Their purrs rumbled through the room.

Sipping the wine, Lamia realised how thirsty she was and quickly asked for water to accompany the wine. She didn't want to become so inebriated her aim became worse!

The Emperor watched her as she drank greedily, following the drop of water that escaped her mouth to roll down her chin and neck. She had originally planned not to eat, but couldn't deny her hunger. With a shrug, she bit into the beef. Eyes closing in appreciation, she couldn't help but let out a moan. It was divine! So tender that it melted on her tongue!

Chatter swelled forth as the court ate. Lost in a new assassination plot, Lamia suddenly became conscious of eyes upon her and looked up to find the lady's eyes still on her.

Lamia smiled nervously and set her knife and fork together.

"You enjoyed your food, Miss Fontaine?" The Emperor asked.

He'd pushed his plate away, leaving a streak of blood upon it.

Lamia glanced over the top of the napkin at him as she dabbed her lips. She didn't want to say anything, but her parents hadn't raised her to be rude. "It was delicious, Your Excellency. Thank you."

He seemed surprised by her politeness and caught the attention of the servant clearing away their plates. "Please send our compliments to the chef. My new wife, Ms Fontaine, was most impressed."

She winced against the word 'wife'.

How in the name of all the gods was she going to get out of this one?!

There was a moment of awkward quiet as the servant left. Lamia squirmed under his gaze as they waited. Moments later, another two servants appeared, carefully wheeling in a trolley with a large multi-tiered cake atop of it. Hand crafted sugar roses covered the cake, their lustrous red stark against the white icing. A knife had been placed on a gold plate beside it.

Renewed determination coursed through her, its euphoria dizzying. She smiled nervously at him, whilst he continued to watch her intently. A round of applause erupted from the courtiers as they rose to their feet.

"Shall we?" The Emperor said, offering her his hand.

She contemplated spitting in it, but her parent's appalled faces appeared once more in her thoughts. Standing with care, she reluctantly accepted it. He was cool to the touch, and a shudder ran through her, rekindling her anger.

Allowing herself to be led over to the table where the cake had been set, he reached for the knife, offering it to her so they could slice the cake together. Snatching it from his hand, she whirled, lunging for his chest, but didn't get far. An arm had locked itself around her waist, pulling her back. She yelped in pain as the guard twisted the blade from her hand.

"Get. Off. My. Wife!" roared the Emperor, yanking the guard off her and throwing him across the hall.

There was a stunned silence as the court watched the guard back away, garbling his apologies. The Felidaeon began circling the Emperor and his new bride.

"No one touches my wife but me. Do you understand?"

And, to emphasise his point, the Emperor pulled her to him, crushing her against his chest in the most intimate of embraces. Her cheeks warmed at the feel of him.

"Now, where were we? Oh yes, you were trying to kill me. Again." He pulled her closer still, fingers caressing her neck with one hand whilst the other accepted a second knife from a servant. "We shall have to find a new game to play, my *dear*," he ground out, breath tickling her ear. "Don't worry. I can think of one or two..."

His honey tones burned through her. She inhaled quickly to banish her dizziness. Heart thundering, she tried to prise herself free only to have him tighten his hold, pressing her ever closer against him. Heat rising in her cheeks to feel the contours of his body flush against her back. She looked away as his hand covered hers and, together, they cut the cake.

The court applauded politely.

She had a knife! Maybe she could—

As if reading her mind, he squeezed her hand in a vice-like hold and she gasped, dropping the knife. He kicked it away, sending it dancing across the floor, then led her firmly out of the dining room. Unable to yank her hand free, she kicked and thumped him as he half-dragged her down a series of corridors and up several flights of stairs, ever deeper into the Black Palace. The Felidaeon padded after them, nipping playfully at servants on their way past.

Luscious white roses lined the black-and-gold marble balustrades. If she hadn't been so busy fighting him, she would've enjoyed the efforts the servants had obviously gone to in their displays, preparing the palace for the Emperor's new bride.

"As much as I like feisty foreplay, Ms Fontaine, this is growing tiresome. Are you going to tell me what makes you so determined to kill me?"

He dragged her towards a set of doors guarded by footmen, his cloak billowing behind him. The Footmen hastily opened the doors for them, expressions neutral as they watched him pull her into a voluptuous suite decorated in white and complete with soft furnishings. An opulent four-poster bed with a white and gold brocaded canopy stood in the centre of the room, whilst a large freestanding bathtub took pride of place in the window overlooking the canals of Dårath far below.

She looked away, cheeks burning. "Rot in hell!"

With a sigh, he nodded for the Footmen to leave them in peace, and Lamia watched in horror as the doors shut behind them.

She was trapped.

As if to emphasise the point, his Felidaeon sat down in front of them. Their amber eyes watching her aloofly as they proceeded to clean themselves, licking their front paws, their tails swishing contentedly.

Quickly putting a settee between them, she looked him over. She hadn't properly looked at him since the Chapel. He looked vexed and weary, and a little sad. He seemed at a loss for what to do. Taking off his cloak, he draped it over a chair as he made his way over to a set of decanters. One rested in ice—blood. She shuddered in distaste. It was from this he poured himself a drink before pouring a generous helping of some honey-coloured liqueur into another crystal tumbler.

Turning, he caught sight of her and a look of pain washed over his fine features. Hesitating for a moment, he crossed the room with the two drinks. He was broad shouldered and carried his height well. Walking toward her with all the grace of a Felidaeon himself, she didn't know whether to run or welcome him. She was utterly entranced, like prey that had sighted the predator and knew not which way to run.

If it weren't for the sadness in his face, she would've run.

I suppose he just wanted a nice day to celebrate finding his new bride; she thought guiltily, before shaking herself. *A creature like him doesn't deserve pity!*

"It is mead," he said shyly, passing her the tumbler. "It was made using the honey from our own bees, collected from the palace gardens."

"You have gardens?" Her earnest expression belaying her interest. She'd tended the garden back home and people often commented on her green thumb. She certainly felt her happiest with her hands in the dirt, lost amongst her plants.

She sighed. She was going to miss her little garden.

He smiled. "Of course. And orchards and farmland and woodland. I find great beauty in nature and have made it a priority for the palace to be self-sufficient, leaving the crops grown on public land for the people of Noxterra. You like gardening?"

"Why make mead if you don't drink it?" she asked, ignoring his question. She sniffed the contents dubiously.

He settled himself on a settee with a sigh, stretching out his long legs. "It is given to the people of Dårath as a gift for the Solstice and Equinox. The human staff enjoy it, too."

She took a sip and wandered cautiously over to the circular window, one eye on him and his Felidaeon. Despite the night sky, the mountains seemed to glow, the moonlight of the twin moons reflecting off their snow-clad tops. The city itself was alight with enchanted lamps. Fireworks exploded far below, scattering their multicoloured dapples across the surface of the canal waters. She could hear the faint echoes of music and laughter: celebrations for the Queen of Noxterra were in full swing.

And, somewhere down there, were her parents...

A pang of sadness washed over her then as she scanned the darkness below.

"They are staying with Baron Fitzroy," he said, as if reading her mind. "I have invited them to attend your official introduction to court tomorrow evening."

"You have?"

He glanced over the rim of his glass at her. "Of course," he said, taking a sip. "They are welcome to move into the palace if they wish. A suite is always available for my wife's family."

"I thought—"

"That you were a prisoner here?" he interrupted, eyes twinkling with mischief. "Whilst The Picking is one of my few stipulations of the people of Noxterra in exchange for protection, I do it to find company, not to wreck lives."

"I'm sure the Emperor can find all the company he needs in Dårath's red quarters," she retorted hotly.

"Company of a sort can be found, true," he said, swirling his drink so it glooped along its sides.

Her insides heaved at the sight of it.

Gods, no, please don't let it be his...

"But not the sort I seek," he continued, unaware of the horror on her face. "I am old and past the wanton antics of youth. Though I am not seeking a love match, the company I enjoy is more *intimate...*"

"As if I could fall in love with a monster like you!" she snapped viciously.

He faltered like a blow had been dealt. After a long moment, he licked his lips. "So," he said, continuing, "in exchange for the 'inconvenience' of becoming my bride, I ensure their families are looked after, whilst also trying to fulfil their *every* wish. A task that occasionally proves more taxing than court business..."

She blushed, happily taking another sip of the mead to avoid meeting his ardent gaze. Standing by the window, she watched the celebrations continue under the cool glow of the twin moons.

"The wedding night is rarely *uneventful*," he said, suddenly appearing behind her.

How had he got there so fast?

She felt his cool fingers untie her chignon as he spoke. "But you have certainly made today my most memorable."

Loosening her hair, he marvelled at its curls, toying with them as he set her glass down and proceeded to kiss the gentle curve of her neck.

She shivered and made to pull away.

"I promise I won't bite," he said, trailing kisses across her skin. "Not tonight, anyway. You are most delicious..."

He was surprisingly gentle and, whilst she tried to keep her mind on the opportunity presenting itself, possibly her last for a while, she was finding it difficult to concentrate on an attack: his touch was markedly warm for a vampire... She'd been kissed plenty of times and had enjoyed some fondling with the neighbours' son, but she had never been touched with such reverence. There was an underlying thrum of delight that was almost tangible. He brushed her throat with his fangs and she let out a gasp as a shiver ran down her spine.

A knock at the door stirred her from the reverie she'd found herself in. Horrified at how close she'd come to being enthralled, she pulled away. With a growl, Emperor Amias barked for the servant to enter.

Shyly, a maid appeared holding out a lacquer tray atop of which were the roses from the Chapel. They were crumpled and in a poor state.

"Thank you. Please leave them on the stand," he said, waving impatiently for her to leave them alone.

The servant weaved her way passed the Felidaeon, which nipped playfully at her ankles, and deposited the tray before quickly exiting.

As the doors closed once more, Amias turned to find Lamia worrying her bottom lip.

"I believe we were getting somewhere quite significant," he said, walking over with purpose, eyes smouldering.

The girl gulped. "I—"

"Don't go getting shy with me now, Lamia," he breathed, pulling her against him.

She shuddered to hear her name on his lips, said like a prayer.

He let the back of his hand trail down her cheeks. She flinched, only to find his touch gentle. His other hand roamed the small of her back, coasting the curves of her derriere and thigh, whilst the other reached her chin, angling it so her lips were a whisper away from his.

Now, Lamia! Focus! She screamed inwardly, but she was lost, lightheaded, as she awaited his lips on hers.

Then she felt his hand trail along her garter.

And brush against the knife.

They looked at each other for a moment in mutual shock, then she lurched into action, trying to snatch the blade from him just as he lifted her skirts to retrieve it. Before she knew what had happened, he'd swung her round, driving her up against the wall, pinning her hands above her head.

He tut-tutted. "Really, my dear, I thought we'd called a truce for the evening."

"Never!" she spat.

He pushed her hands more firmly against the wall. She let out a gasp of pain, her back arching under him. A groan escaped his mouth at the touch of her body below his, eyes narrowing as they roved over the curves of her lips, and neck, and bosom.

"I wish you would tell me," he said, voice surprisingly emotional.

Blinking, she mustered her final bit of strength to glare at him.

"I could make you," he whispered, pressing himself ever closer, so his body covered hers.

Her heart stopped at the feel of his arousal, hard through the netting and lace of her skirts.

His purple gaze locked with hers in a breathtaking moment. His eyes seemed to glow. "I could compel you."

"To have sex with you?!" she snarled, cheeks red as she kicked out at him, trying to wrench away.

He contemplated the notion, dodging her heel. "I would rather not. It is *far* more pleasurable when it is given freely... No, to tell me. To tell me why you hate me so."

"Why would a murderer like you care?" she grounded out, acutely aware of the feel of him. Her heart hammered painfully against her chest, which rose quickly as she tried to steady her breath, brushing him.

To her surprise, he moaned, eyes fluttering shut as if he were regaining composure. He breathed in deeply, nostrils flaring, and when he opened his eyes again, they smouldered.

"A lot. Surprisingly. Though I promised myself I wouldn't. Not this time. It hurts so... But, from the moment I saw you enter the Chapel, I hoped it would be you. Of all the maidens I've seen these past few days, none stood out like you. You shine as if you are a star of Målilore, fallen from the heavens." His voice was a soft purr that pulsed through her. "And rulers don't acquire their power without some blood loss."

"I wasn't referring to—"

He reached for the knife in her garter, cool fingers trickling up her thigh, stopping just short of her undergarments as he removed it. The heat that melted her core was unlike any she had felt before.

Speechless, she could do nothing as he leaned ever closer until his lips were but a breath from hers. The insane urge to feel them on hers, to rake her hands through his long raven-black hair, was overwhelming. All she could see was him. He filled her vision.

"So, tell me, what are you referring to? Why are you more intent on killing me than bedding me?"

She looked away, cheeks reddening.

"I know you want to. Underneath everything. I can sense your desire... I can smell it..."

She rose her chin in defiance, but avoided his gaze all the same.

Fetching out the knife, he let go of her hands to bend the blade as easily as if it were parchment. He carefully blunted its edges before placing it on the side. He then unbuttoned his jerkin.

Lamia blushed, folding her arms in front of her defensively. "What are you—"

"I think you owe me a wedding present. To say sorry."

"A what?! But, I have nothing!"

He sat down, jerkin undone, revealing the tough contours of his abdomen. "Well, I can always sit and watch and you can always—"

"I'm not one of those girls," she said, cutting in.

"Oh, I think you are..." He spread his legs wide. "And I think you could put on quite a show."

She stared at him in disbelief; the heat rising in her cheeks.

He waited expectantly, an unmistakable bulge at his crotch.

After what seemed an age, her mind whirling as to what to do, he let out a sigh.

"It's late. If you shall not talk with me, nor play for me, nor bed me, I shall rest." He stood to remove his crown, shrugging his jerkin to the floor.

Unable to resist, she sneaked a look at his lean torso and sculpted chest, long dark hair flowing down his back. Though his chest was bare, there was a treasure trail leading below the waistband of his breeches. Feeling heat explode within her abdomen, she tore her eyes away to find him watching her with unbridled desire. Unbuttoning his breeches carefully, he let them fall and she inhaled at the size of his cock.

He leisurely pulled on a pair of braies which did nothing but emphasise the delights below. She gulped and felt herself lick her dry lips.

"There is only one bed though, wife. Will you join me?" He pulled back the covers.

She cleared her throat. "I shall sleep on the settee, Your Excellency."

As you wish," he sighed with a pout. "And, if you must use a title, at least acknowledge our new relationship. Call me 'My Lord'. Or, better yet, 'dear heart.'"

Lamia scoffed before remembering herself. She regarded him coolly. "As you wish, *My Lord*."

With a grumble, he shuffled under the covers and tapped the torch beside the bed, plunging the room into darkness.

Moonlight filtered through the circular window, casting a cool glow upon the room and its interior. As Lamia settled on the long settee, bundling the skirts of her dress about her for warmth, she was aware of his purple gaze on her, glowing through the dark, boring into her.

Never had she felt more alone or trapped.

Overwhelmed by the day's events, she couldn't stop tears of despair from falling before drifting off into a troubled sleep.

5

New Reality

Though she fell into a troubled sleep only after the moons had passed their zenith, she woke early. Faint sunlight glimmered through the stain glass, sprinkling shards of colour across the chamber. She was surprisingly warm and found someone had covered her with the bed sheets during the night.

Maybe placed there by Amias?

Sitting up to yawn, she glanced over to find the bed empty. Stunned, she looked around the suite. It was empty and his clothes were gone.

"Your Excellency? I mean, 'My Lord'?" she said cautiously, pulling the sheets off her to get up.

Nothing. She was totally alone.

He'd left her?!

She shouldn't have been surprised, not after how she'd been towards him. She denied him her company as a wife, something her mother had insisted she must do if she were chosen. Though her mind had been too busy plotting his death to pay much heed to her mother's advice.

Battling a wave of unexpected sadness, she jumped when a knock sounded on the door.

"Come in!" Lamia called, smoothing her skirts.

A head peeked round. It was the servant from the previous night, the one who'd brought her the roses.

She noticed the drooping blooms with guilt for the first time, having completely forgotten about them.

"Good morning, Your Majesty. My name's Theodora. His Excellency has appointed me as your Maid-in-Waiting." The girl curtsied.

She appeared about Lamia's age, with chestnut coloured hair, a dusting of freckles and the pointed ears of a Fæ. Horns curved round from her temples. Her smile was warm and genuine, and Lamia immediately liked her.

"Hello, Theodora. It's nice to meet you," Lamia said with a shy smile.

"Emperor Amias is in the Central Court attending to matters and requested I helped you prepare. Should you like me to run you a bath?" Theodora asked, spying the bundle of sheets on the settee and the crumpled knife on the side.

If she was surprised, she didn't show it.

"Yes please," Lamia said. She hadn't washed since the morning previous and hated to think how she must smell.

The girl went over to the bath at the window and turned some gold knobs on its side. There was a gurgle and water gushed out.

Lamia ran over in surprise. "Water?!"

Theodora smiled as she covered a hole with a plug and sprinkled some sweet-smelling salts into the water. "The Emperor is always looking for ways to make life easier for everyone. This water is collected from the rain and warmed by the sun. He designed the system himself. New buildings in Dårath are being built with the necessary tanks and pipework, and he is encouraging other cities to follow suit. It saves so much time and effort!"

Rose scented steam drifted from the bath, and Theodora helped Lamia out of her gown.

"What a beautiful dress, Your Majesty!"

"Thank you. My mother had it made for... for The Picking..." Lamia trailed off. Her previous life felt so distant from her new reality.

"It must feel ever so strange, Your Majesty. If you don't mind me saying."

Lamia smiled sadly over at her. "Yes, it does."

There was another knock at the door, and Lamia reached for a sheet to cover her chemise and stay.

"That'll be the seamstress," Theodora said, crossing to open the door.

Several women entered, carrying several garments and a sewing box. Whilst Theodora finished the bath, the seamstress amended several dresses, making the necessary adjustments so they fitted her curves perfectly.

"They're stunning!" Lamia gasped, feeling the material in wonder. Though her father had afforded excellent clothing for them, she'd never seen such fine needlework.

The seamstress blushed. "Thank you, Your Majesty. You're very kind. His Excellency chose the designs."

Lamia looked surprised. "He did?"

"Oh yes," she said, passing the gown to one of her attendants, who began making the final adjustments. "He has a fine eye. He also put in a request for a gown for you this morning before he attended court, but I'm afraid it shan't be ready until this evening. I have my girls working on it now."

"Oh, thank you. I'm sorry to cause you trouble."

"Not at all, Your Majesty. The Emperor was keen for you to wear it for your parents this evening."

Lamia gasped. She'd forgotten that Amias had invited her parents to attend that evening's ceremony. Her heart warmed at the thought of seeing them again.

"The bath is ready, Your Majesty," Theodora announced, gesturing for the seamstress and the other two servants to tidy up their things and depart.

Once alone, Theodora helped Lamia remove her stay and chemise, producing clean ones with elaborate brocade work.

Lamia sank into the hot water with a sigh, beginning to wash herself with the scrubs and lotions that Theodora had left out for her. Theodora chatted amiably whilst she prepared a red gown for Lamia to change into. It had an intricate gold trim around its neckline and cuffs.

"I hope you don't mind me asking, but are you from Elphyne?" Lamia asked, as Theodora poured water over her hair to rinse it clean.

"Yes, Your Majesty. I entered His Excellency's household to help repay his kindness in appointing my father Baron of Glenwood."

"I've heard of Glenwood. It's part of the Unseelie Court, isn't it? And you don't mind working here?" She'd heard all sorts of rumours of the Unseelie Court, of their cunning and cruelty, and was amazed to find Theodora so pleasant.

"No, it's an honour to represent my family so. The Fæ have long served the Emperor since he originally came from Elphyne himself. He once ruled the Unseelie Court prior to arriving in Noxterra, but his brother's descendants now rule in his stead. You will meet them later. Though, speaking plain, Your Majesty, I do miss the green of the forest and hills," she sighed.

"Isn't the Unseelie Court also known as the Winter Court?"

"Only because its rulers are blessed with Winter's Kiss."

Theodora stopped by the roses on their silver tray.

"I'm afraid I was too distracted to tend to the flowers last night," Lamia admitted guiltily.

"Not to worry," Theodora said, fetching out a vase from a cupboard and filling it with water from a basin.

Once dry, Lamia put on the gown with Theodora's help. There was a mirror on the wall opposite the window and Lamia gazed in amazement at her reflection. Never had she looked more like a queen and less like Lamia Fontaine of Garren. The red silk brocade hugged her figure, showing off the curve of her hips, whilst the plunging neckline emphasised the swell of her breasts. Its skirts puddled on to the floor, trailing a little in her wake. Her sleeves were red gossamer and decorated with several bands of gold trim.

"You don't think this is a little much?" Lamia asked, turning on the spot. "I feel like I ought to be going to a ball and not just a walk around the palace."

"His Excellency will want you looking your best whether you are walking around the palace or sitting reading a book, Your Majesty. He has commissioned these gowns and more just for you."

Sitting at the dressing table, Theodora worked her magic on Lamia's makeup and curls before draping a delicate golden headpiece down its parting to rest upon her forehead. An embossed rose decorated its middle pendant. Fastening a large ruby pendant around her neck, Theodora took a step back.

"Perfect. Are you ready to make your appearance at court, Your Majesty?"

THE DARK OF THE PALACE was stark after the lightness of the suite. Following Theodora along the maze of corridors, they passed servants busy with their chores, smiling to one another and humming as they worked. Several members of court paraded past in their finery. One was the woman with blonde hair that Lamia had noticed. She was standing with another lady deep in conversation when they spied Lamia walking with Theodora. Quickly stepping forward, the lady curtsied and Lamia stopped to return the curtsy.

"It's an honour to meet you, Your Majesty. My name is Lady Visha Dunbarrow, daughter of Baron Dunbarrow. You look exquisite! And *so* well!"

"Thank you. It's lovely to meet you, Lady Visha."

Lady Visha bowed her head humbly, eyes looking demurely through her lashes, but when they rose to meet hers, there was a touch of frost to them.

"I trust you had a pleasant evening. You disappeared *so* suddenly."

Lamia blushed at the memory of her failed attack in the dining room. "I did, thank you," she stammered. "I needed the rest after such a long day."

Lady Visha raised a brow, a smug smile tugging her lips. "I can imagine."

There was a slight pause as the Lady Visha's gaze roved over her, taking in the golden headpiece and her fine gown.

"I hope you won't be disappointed..."

Taken aback, Lamia found Lady Visha's eyes gleaming with malice.

"But, judging from yesterday, love isn't what you're looking for..."

With that, Lady Visha excused herself and continued on her way down the corridor. Her friend gave an embarrassed curtsy before quickly hurrying off after her.

What was that all about?

AMIAS SHIFTED IN HIS throne and turned his wandering thoughts back to the gentleman presenting in front of him with difficulty. It had been like this all morning. Unusually for him, he had found his concentration lacking, with it frequently turning to his new bride and not on the matters of state being presented to him. Not that he understood why. He had hoped to have consummated their marriage last night. Perhaps that was why he couldn't concentrate? Brides were usually prudent, which was a commendable characteristic, but none had refused him on their wedding night. Indeed, most had quickly given in to the pleasure. Maybe Lamia had been hoping for a love match. But then, she'd made it perfectly clear she didn't want one either. Certainly not with him. That she would rather see him at the end of her knife than inside her.

Murderer...

He shuddered involuntarily at the memory. If she hadn't been referring to deaths on the battlefield, whose had she been referring to? But, more importantly, why did he care?

And that infuriated him. More than he wanted to admit.

There was a commotion at the entrance to the Central Court. The guards on duty had lowered their halberds, blocking the way into the vaulted room. A woman dressed in a red silk gown was there. The guards were questioning her, their voices gruff.

At first, he didn't recognise her. All he was aware of was the world slowing until it stood still. A sensation he hadn't felt since he had first laid eyes upon his first wife. The one who had known the real him. The one he had loved...

Shaking himself from his reverie, it was then he recognised her: Lamia...

She looked totally different dressed in the gown and such finery. Seeing her detained so, seeing the guards treat her roughly, filled him with an uncontrollable rage, unlike any he'd experienced in years. Before he knew what he was doing, he was storming down the dais and across the courtroom, much to the surprise of those in attendance. His three Felidaeon immediately followed him, hackles raised, sensing his change in temper.

On hearing his approach, the guards spun round, eyes widening to see him so enraged.

"Your Ex—"

"Hands off my wife! Nobody touches her! Do you understand?!" he roared.

He was speaking louder than he intended, bellowing even, but he couldn't stop himself. Despite knowing members of the public were watching, let alone his courtiers. All he could see was red rage. And

Lamia, looking beautiful and stunned and vulnerable as he pushed the guards aside to stand protectively in front of her.

Talon growing, fangs lengthening, he poised himself to fight. "I'll rip out the throats of any who lay but a finger on her, and I shall gladly drink you dry!"

There was an uneasy silence as the guards scrambled away from the snarling Felidaeon. Bowing profusely, they snivelled their apologies.

Without waiting to gauge their reaction, Amias whirled round, and, grabbing Lamia's wrist, he strode down the corridor and away.

LAMIA STRUGGLED TO keep up with him despite the Felidaeon nipping playfully at her ankles. He was at least a head taller than her, and his stride was that much greater. Tripping over her own feet, she righted herself just before she fell flat on her face. It was only then that he slowed. But he still avoided looking at her. His eyes, which had turned a glaring red as he'd confronted the guards, had yet to return to their usual purple. Without a word, he directed her through a set of doors at the end of the corridor, before pulling her through another set to reveal the dining room.

Full of courtiers breaking their fast, they shot to their feet on seeing the Emperor and Lamia. Murmured greetings and bows followed in their wake as he led her towards where Lady Visha sat.

Lady Visha rose elegantly to her feet and curtsied, her eyes piqued with curiosity.

"My Lord," she murmured demurely, noticing his blazing eyes.

If Emperor Amias found her address familiar, he didn't show it.

"I have state business still to attend to. Please, may you tend to my wife in my absence?"

"Of course, My Lord," she said, lips curling into a sultry smile.

He hesitated then, eyes flickering to purple. He seemed about to say something, but caught Lamia's eye and thought better of it. Lady

Visha curtsied again, even lower than before. Without another word, he left, sweeping through another door, his Felidaeon trotting behind him. The court rose in farewell.

Left alone, Lamia was grateful when the attention of everyone in the room refocused on breakfast.

Smiling shyly, Lamia took her place next to Lady Visha and began helping herself to toast and honey, spreading plenty of butter on before spooning on the honey.

"Would you like some tea, Your Majesty?" Lady Visha asked, reaching for a large china teapot.

"Yes, thank you," Lamia said, grateful for some normality after the Emperor's odd outburst.

"You must be famished."

With a smirk, Lady Visha poured the tea. The steaming red drink sploshed messily over the teacup's sides.

"Oh, dear! Clumsy me!" Lady Visha exclaimed, tilting the teapot some more to spill its hot contents across the table and Lamia's wrist.

With a cry of surprise, Lamia whipped her hand away. The burn throbbed painfully. Wincing, Lamia glanced from the patch of red, taut skin to Lady Visha's conceited face.

"Opps!" gasped Lady Visha, covering her mouth in mock dismay. "Accidents can happen *so* easily here."

The doors reopened and the courtiers, expecting the Emperor, rose quickly to their feet. Lamia noticed a look of panic wash over Lady Visha's face as she hastily pushed the teapot away.

It was Theodora.

With a sigh of relief, Lamia was about to go to her when Lady Visha grabbed her burnt wrist, squeezing it tight.

Lamia let out a gasp of pain as Lady Visha clenched her harder and pulled her close. "Breathe a word to anyone, and you will wish you weren't born," she spat.

Lady Visha released her grip with a cruel smile and watched Lamia hasten to the Fæ girl.

ONCE THEODORA HAD TENDED to Lamia's burn, cleansing it and covering it with a gauze dressing, she led Lamia to a south-facing parlour. It was a large room with a stunning bay window that gave out onto the gardens. Its walls were painted a deep jade, with intricate carvings that sparkled in gold leaf. It was comfortably furnished with plush settees, armchairs, loveseats and a writing desk. Lamia instantly fell in love with it. Though the air was musty from disuse.

"This room has always traditionally been allocated for the Queen's private use. If it pleases you, Your Majesty, you may use it too. I shall ask Rûntal to select a suitable guard to keep watch and ensure unwanted visitors stay away."

Lamia, who had crossed over to the bay window to gaze out upon the gardens, smiled gratefully. "Thank you. I'd appreciate that."

Theodora opened a window to let in some fresh air and approached the door. She hesitated on her way out. "I'm sorry, Your Majesty. When I heard he'd left you in that bitch's care, I got to you as soon as I could. I trust you shall inform His Excellency of Lady Visha's misdemeanour."

Lamia stiffened and glanced briefly down at the bandage about her wrist. Pulling the sleeve to cover it, she then smiled brightly. "No, it was an accident. He wouldn't want to be bothered by such trivialities."

Theodora didn't look convinced. Nonetheless, she inclined her head and curtsied. "As you wish, Your Majesty."

And Theodora closed the door behind her, leaving Lamia alone to her thoughts.

6

Hall of Mirrors

Agitated beyond reason, Amias could not return to the Central Court, cancelling the remaining cases until the next week. Deciding he wasn't in the mood for company, he made his way to his study. The High Priest had other plans and was hovering in the corridor when he emerged.

"I trust you spent a pleasant evening with your new bride," the High Priest said with barely contained excitement as he fell into step beside the Emperor.

Amias cut him a sidelong look.

A Felidaeon nipped the corner of the High Priest's cloak, tearing a hole in it.

"Heel, Astro," Amias said, reaching for the Felidaeon.

Undeterred, the High Priest continued buoyantly. "The Picking chose well for you this time, Your Excellency. Your new queen is most becoming!"

Amias couldn't deny that, so gave a curt nod of agreement.

"I can see why you already dote on her so."

"I do not dote!" he snapped, purple eyes flashing as he approached the guards on duty at his study.

The High Priest gave a knowing smile. "No, Your Excellency. Of course not. I'm sure she will settle in soon enough and become a great asset to Noxterra."

"I'm sure she will," Amias agreed gruffly.

The door was opened for him, and Amias settled himself behind his desk. One of the Felidaeon hesitated at the door, before continuing to pad down the corridor. The remaining two settled in front of the fire, tucking their enormous paws under them as they got comfy. Glancing up at the High Priest, he waited impatiently for him to say anything further.

With a little chuckle, the High Priest bowed and excused himself.

IT WASN'T LONG BEFORE there was a knock at the door.

Lamia hadn't moved from the bay window, still lost in thought as she gazed over the gardens. A determined frown upon her brow as she let this new reality wash over her.

"Come in," she called, reluctantly turning.

A knight entered wearing a black tunic with a gold rose over his heart: The Queen's Guard. The Emperor assigned The Guard and The Knights of Eternal Darkness, rumoured to be his vampire offspring, to safeguard the Queen and Royal Household.

The man was pale with dark hair and pointed ears. Lamia was surprised to see he had purple eyes like the Emperor—perhaps this was another rumour that was true and this was a son of his? Though he wasn't in full battle armour, he still cut an impressive figure with the curves of his muscles visible through his tunic. A broad sword hung from a belt at his waist.

He bowed low on seeing her. A large Felidaeon was at his heels, its whiskers twitching as it sniffed the air.

Was it one of the Emperor's?

"Greetings, Your Majesty. My name is Rûntal, Captain of The Queen's Guard. Theodora said you had need of a guard." He stepped aside and a burly man dressed in identical attire appeared, bowing. "This is Hezron. I have assigned him to you."

"It is an honour to serve you, Your Majesty!" Hezron said, bowing low once more.

He was of a similar build to Rûntal, but had mousey blonde hair, though his eyes were the same purple.

Lamia curtsied back. "Thank you. It's a pleasure to make your acquaintance."

"Is there anything else I can get you?" Rûntal asked, gesturing for Hezron to take up position outside of the door. "Allow none but myself, Theodora and father to enter."

"On my life!" Hezron placed a hand over his heart and bowed before leaving to stand guard.

So, the rumours were right!

Lamia felt a flash of triumph before fear chilled her. *If that was true, how many more rumours were true? And did that make him her stepson?!*

Feeling Rûntal's eyes on her, she stammered. "I would appreciate a writing set. I should like to write to my parents."

"Of course, Your Majesty. I shall get Theodora to bring one up for you." He turned to leave, but hesitated at the door. "Father intends to present you officially at court tomorrow, but I could arrange a tour of the palace for you this afternoon whilst he attends to official state matters?"

"Yes, that would be lovely, thank you."

Smiling, Rûntal bowed and closed the door behind him.

Left alone once more, Lamia crossed over to where the writing desk was positioned against the wall and sat in its chair. She opened its cover and excitedly inspected the myriad of tiny drawers and cupboards within. Sadly, all were empty. Looking up, she frowned in dissatisfaction with her view of the wall and looked around for inspiration. It was then she spied the bay window. Pulling the chair aside, she proceeded to drag the desk over to the window, positioning it so she could see the gardens. If she was going to be stuck here for the foreseeable future, she wanted a decent view. It was then she noticed doors in the bay window. She was about to try them when the door to the Parlour opened and Theodora appeared with a lacquer writing set.

Lamia hastily dropped her hands to her side.

Theodora did a double take when she saw the newly positioned desk. She gave an amused smile. "I see you're making yourself at home?"

Lamia sniffed. "I wanted a nice view."

"Well, you certainly have that. Though, the gardens aren't as well tended as they used to be," she sighed, placing the box down on the open desk.

"Oh?" Lamia asked, interest piqued.

Theodora smiled over at her. "You like gardening, Your Majesty?"

Lamia blushed and glanced back at the grounds. "Yes, I looked after the garden back home. I'm going to miss it..."

"I am sure the Emperor would welcome your guidance in overseeing the gardens here at the palace. He enjoys nature, and woodland walks, but is not a gardener."

"I can tell," she smiled, "the gardens are lacking the grandeur of the palace."

"So, you like the palace?"

Lamia hesitated. "It's certainly impressive. Rûntal said he was going to organise a tour for me this afternoon..."

Catching the hint, Theodora curtsied. "It would be an honour to assist."

"Thank you. That would be lovely," Lamia said with a shy smile.

"Excellent! Well, in that case, I shall find Rûntal and arrange for lunch to be served for you here, Your Majesty."

"Thank you, Theodora," Lamia said, taking her seat at the writing desk.

"It'll be my pleasure, Your Majesty. Is that all?" Theodora asked, hands clasped before her.

"Yes, thank you."

With a final curtsy, Theodora left.

The lacquer writing set before her was of the finest craftmanship and bore marks of the King of Shangri-La. Lamia assumed it had been a gift. It was the most exquisite thing she'd ever seen and was hand painted with demons and heroes from Shangri-La's legends. There was a tiny key with a leather tassel in its lock. Carefully unlocking it with a satisfying *click!* it unfolded to reveal a writing slope with a red leather tooled sciver. There were compartments near the lock for bits and bobs and an inkwell. Lamia lifted the slope to reveal a sealed ink well, blotting pad, glass pen, parchment, letter opener, and rose-shaped seal with wax.

She eyed the mother-of-pearl letter opener.

The previous blades had inflicted no damage. So, why bother?

But it might. A new opportunity might present itself. With better results. And, at the very least, she could stab out one of those purple eyes of his.

She could almost see them before her, dazzling with their violet hues. Contrasting *perfectly* against the raven black of his hair... Guarded, as if he was protecting something... There was a depth to them that seemed to stretch through time and space. It was staggering to think of everything he must have seen in all those years... What was it like?

Why did she care?!

With an impatient sniff, she pulled herself from her reverie and took up the letter opener. Hitching up her skirts, she placed it back in her garter. The feel of its cool blade against her skin was immediately reassuring. Smoothing down her skirts, she fetched out the ink well, a glass pen and a sheet of parchment. Closing the slope, Lamia arranged her writing equipment and began her letter.

AMIAS STARED AT THE untouched scrolls of parchment before him. He wasn't aware how long he'd been sat there, staring into space, but he knew it had been long enough.

Why had he lost his temper so? And in front of all those people?!

He massaged his brow and sighed.

Murderer...

He couldn't get her voice out of his head. He couldn't unsee those brilliant blue eyes of hers, shining with all the ferocity of the Atlantean sea.

Mind made up, he tossed the papers aside and crossed the room. He was going to find his wife.

AFTER HAVING EATEN a delicious lunch of roast goat and spring vegetables, Theodora had arrived to begin their tour of the palace. She began at the beginning, returning Lamia to the main entranceway, with its grand butterfly staircase and chandelier. Afternoon light poured through the gigantic stained-glass window, sparkling off the black crystal chandelier like fairy dust. From there, she showed Lamia the way to the Central Court and State Rooms beyond, including the Dining Room, Gallery, Ballroom and Music Room. She then showed her shortcuts out from the State Rooms, ones to her Parlour and others to her Chambers, too. Perfect for a quick escape. All the while, Hezron followed, walking at a respectful distance.

It was as Theodora led her to the Chapel that the nearest room's doors were flung open and out came Emperor Amias. Two Felidaeon trailed behind him.

Eyes falling on Lamia, he stopped short in shock, as if he'd just witnessed a dream come true. He gazed at her, overcome, his violet eyes shining.

Theodora quickly curtsied and, casting Lamia a pointed look, Lamia copied, sweeping the skirts of her gown so they pooled around her. Behind her, she could hear Hezron fall to his knee.

"Your Excellency! I was just giving the Queen a tour of the palace."

Pulling himself together, Amias looked around with a quizzical brow. "Where is Lady Visha?"

Theodora hesitated, clasping her hands together, their knuckles whitening.

"Sadly, she had some family business to attend to," Lamia said quickly. "She was most attentive."

This seemed to satisfy him. "What are you doing here, Hezron?"

"The guard rose to his feet and placed a hand over his heart. "Rûntal assigned me as the Queen's personal guard, father."

"Excellent." Bowing suddenly, Amias offered Lamia his hand. "Allow me to help finish the tour."

Lamia stared at it in confusion, glancing over at Theodora. With a jerk of her head, she motioned for Lamia to take it.

Feeling the familiar stab of pain and hatred, she gulped down her tart retort and accepted it.

"We were going to the Hall of Mirrors next, Your Excellency."

"Perfect, then let us go to the Hall of Mirrors."

And without another word, he swept her off down the corridor. Leaving Theodora and Hezron to trail after them.

CORRIDOR AFTER CORRIDOR sped by them. She would've said she knew exactly where they were, but she didn't. She was helplessly lost. All she was aware of was her hand on his. His touch. It felt cool and hot all at the same time. So much so her hand tingled from the contact. She caught those purple eyes of his looking at her and blushed to see she'd remembered their hues perfectly.

"Didn't you have state matters to attend to, My Lord?" she stammered, her throat dry.

He shifted his eyes away. "I grew tired of state matters."

She stumbled after him, feet tripping over themselves. Glancing nervously at the Felidaeon that trotted by their side. She was relieved to see that this time the big cats were more interested in nipping at passers-by's ankles rather than her own.

They passed through an art gallery where exquisite portraits and landscapes adorned the walls. Marble statues of heroes from Myrrithian legends were scattered around the floor space, along with more vases and curios from the land's many kingdoms.

Doors opened for them and he pulled her into a grand hall lined with floor-to-ceiling mirrors on every wall. He spun her, chuckling to see her surprised face reflected from all angles. The mirrors did not hold his reflection. Looking up, she tore her gaze from the opulent chandelier with its glistening crystals and gasped to see mirrors covering the ceiling.

Shutting the doors behind them, his eyes met her. A playful glint still brightened them.

"Let us take a turn of the room," he suggested, lips still quirked in a smile.

Hand in his, she felt him lead her in step beside him as they walked around the room. Everywhere glistened and shone. With a click of his fingers, enchanted torches came alive in their sconces. The mirrors scattered their brightness, setting the room aglow. She tried not to gape, but it was the most marvellous room she'd ever been in.

"I trust you slept well, My Queen?" he asked after a moment's silence. "I hope you were warm enough."

She glanced up at him, cheeks reddening at the memory of the sheets he'd placed on her. "Yes, My Lord. Very well."

"Good, I'm pleased to hear it." He smiled a knowing smile, meeting her eyes for the briefest of seconds before glancing away. "The gown is most becoming on you."

"Thank you, My Lord."

He cleared his throat. "I used this room for private functions and balls. Though I have had little need for it these past years, I feel we shall use it much more from now on."

Amias suddenly stopped and bowed. "May I have this dance?"

Lamia looked around with a sceptical brow.

"Oh, come now! Don't tell me you're shy! Not after your antics yesterday! Besides," he said, his voice dropping to a velvety purr, "we're totally alone."

Despite herself, she felt warmth rise within her to colour her cheeks.

Without waiting for her reply, he spun her to face him, hands finding her waist. She gulped as her chest bumped against his. Keeping one hand firmly at her waist, he let his other trail up her free arm until their fingers brushed one another. A tingle ran down her arm at the contact, skittering across her heart and down her spine. She shuddered.

"Cold? I know ways to warm you up."

And he led her in a dance around the room. The sparkling light from the sconces was dazzling as he danced her slowly around the room, turning them this way and that with ease. She had been looking forward to treading on his toes and was annoyed to find that, apart from one occasion, she didn't. He was the perfect partner and led with confidence, succeeding to calmly anticipate any poorly placed footing. His raven hair hung loose, flickering in the breeze as they spun around the room. He raised his hand and twirled her, bright eyes watching her and her movements hungrily. Noticing his exposed side, her mind turned to the letter opener in her garter.

He would guess what she was up to if she stopped to hitch up her skirts. She needed him to be helping remove their obstruction to warrant access. She needed to seduce him.

If it meant vengeance on *his* murderer, then so be it.

Amias was still twirling her. Letting a shy giggle escape her lips, she threw herself into another twirl, catching him off guard and losing her footing. He caught her hand, pulling her away from the floor and crushing her against his chest.

They were inches apart.

She felt the breath hitch in her throat and gasped as a jolt ran through her. Heart thundering, she looked up into his eyes, which were feverishly bright. The proximity was intoxicating. A look of absolute astonishment was on his face. Eyes flickering over her fine features as they drank her in.

She gulped. Left breathless with her mind reeling, she gazed blankly up at him.

"Are you alright?" he asked, voice thick with emotion.

She nodded, unable to speak, and watched as his attention flickered from her to her lips. She could almost hear her insides moan as a hunger appeared deep within their purple depths.

A hand appeared to brush away a curl of hair. Her skin burned at the contact. "Have I told you how beautiful you are? Like a goddess incarnate."

"Thank you, My Lord," she stammered, eyes wide with wonder.

Seduce him, damn it! Seduce him!

Not that she really knew how.

Would kissing him be too suspicious?

She tilted her head ever so slightly, allowing her lips to lean closer. She was relieved to find his head move in response. Feeling him a whisper away, she glanced from his lips to his eyes, mesmerising in their intensity. They closed, and she felt his lips take hers. An involuntarily moan escaped her, and she found her eyes closing in bliss.

The kiss was gentle, with a promise of more to come. Something deep inside her yearned to learn what it was, and she found herself kissing him back. Hard. Desperate to know what it was. To feel it. She couldn't stop. The need was insatiable. To have those soft lips whip her into a storm. To have his body firm against hers.

What was she supposed to be doing again?

He was cold beneath her fingertips. As cool and as perfect as the marble statues they'd seen. It was the cold that startled her, knocking sense back to into her. Her eyes flicked open in horror. Quickly fumbling with her skirts, she reached for the letter opener.

"My, you are an eager thing," he breathed, hand following hers, chasing it up her skirts.

The feel of his hand on her thigh sent frissons down her spine and she inhaled, body instinctively arching beneath him.

He moaned as his hand closed around hers, and the letter opener.

Freezing, he looked down to find the blade tucked in her garter, his look of horror turning to amusement.

"A letter opener?" he turned to her in disbelief, his mirth barely contained. "Really, wife, don't you think this is getting a little cliché?"

Lamia found her terror at being found out turn to indignation. She huffed and scowled up at him; the heat rising in her cheeks. "Sorry, there seems to be a lack of stakes in the palace."

His mirth only increased, and he looked at her, his eyes mischievous. "I'll mention it to the staff."

Pushing him away, she crossed her arms, avoiding his eyes.

Taking the letter opener in his hand, he twirled its point against his thumb and cleared his throat. "Out of interest... Who did I kill? Why do you call me a murderer?"

His words struck home, and she couldn't stop the tears from springing up in her eyes. She looked away.

He took a step towards her. "It matters, Lamia. I—"

He stilled, eyes falling on her wrist. The little colour that remained in his complexion vanished instantly.

Her eyes followed his to the dressing now exposed on her wrist.

He seemed unable to talk. Colour returned to his cheeks, bright and hot, and a hardness took over his purple gaze.

"Who did that to you?" His voice came out coarse and thin. He strode over to her, eyes positively blazing, and despite the anger that rolled off him like black thunder, his touch was gentle as it lifted her elbow. He gently pulled the gauze aside, revealing the hideous burn that pocked her skin. A hiss escaped his lips.

"Who did that to you?" he repeated in deadly tones.

Part of her wanted to tell him. To see what he would do, but Lady Visha's threat rang in her ears. She looked away. "No one. I did it to myself. It was an accident."

He snarled, the sound rumbling from the back of his throat. He bent close, his nostrils flaring as if he could smell the lie. "No one touches you, do you understand? You are the Queen of Noxterra: *My* Queen. No one touches *my* queen and treats her like this!"

Red flared in the depths of his eyes and, before she could say anything, he turned and yelled. "Theodora!"

Within seconds, the doors had opened and Theodora rushed in. Looking around her, her eyes rested on where they stood. She noticed the Emperor holding up Lamia's wounded wrist in one hand, and the letter opener in the other. Then she saw his eyes and froze.

"Take my queen to our chambers and use that ointment to tend to this wound. Get her ready for this evening's presentation at court. I shall meet you at the Throne Room."

Theodora curtsied low. "Y-yes, Your Excellency!"

And, without another word or a backward glance, he stormed off, slamming the door shut behind him. There was a splintering sound as cracks appeared in the mirrors surrounding the doorframe.

7

Second Chance

Ordering some of 'that ointment' from the servant at the door, Theodora then led Lamia out and up the endless corridors and staircases to her chambers. Hezron followed after at a smart pace, eyes alert. Lamia could tell the Fæ girl was desperate to ask her what had happened, but was astute enough to remain quiet until after they were back in the state chamber.

"I've never seen him so angry!" she proclaimed once the chamber doors had clicked shut behind them. She rushed over to the bath and turned the knobs. Hot water sploshed into the tub. "He found your wound?"

Lamia watched her sprinkle some sweet-smelling salts into the bath. "We were dancing and then..." she blushed, "then he noticed the bandage."

"Did you tell him it was her?"

"No, of course not! She told me not to."

Theodora's eyes flashed. "You should have. Lady Visha's a snake in the grass. You don't owe her any loyalty, Your Majesty. And why did His Excellency have the letter opener from your writing set? You weren't trying to kill him again?"

Lamia looked away in embarrassment. "You know about that?"

"Everyone knows!" Theodora clucked her tongue. "You need to stop this foolishness, Your Majesty!"

Lamia started at the abruptness in Theodora's voice.

The Fæ girl carried on, though, this time her tone was softer. "You are now his bride. It probably wasn't the future you envisaged, but it is the truth. Whether you want it or not. It is the undeniable truth. You made the roses bloom. You cannot pretend it didn't happen." She glanced over at the roses in their vase, still crumpled and sorry looking. "You are destined to be his. By the gods' design or some greater will, you were destined to be here, by his side and now. It is a great honour, for you and your family. You need not worry about food, warmth, clothing or anything anymore. For as long as you live. You might not even need to worry about love. It's plain to see how taken the Emperor is with you—and that will only grow."

Lamia was about to interrupt. To tell her that he didn't want a love match, that she was wrong, but Theodora pushed on.

"You are lucky. He could easily have you killed for your disobedience."

"I wish he would!" Lamia cried, tears blurring her vision as the failure of her assassination efforts hit her. Along with the familiar sense of loss. "I have nothing to live for!"

Theodora wiped a tear away, placing her hand on Lamia's shoulder. "You don't mean that..."

The girl didn't answer, and the Fæ took in the grief that cut her deep and wondered.

When Theodora spoke again, it was with such gentleness, Lamia cried anew. "You do. You might not see it now, but you do. You have so much to live for. Learn to accept it graciously and think of ways to repay it forward. If not for him, for others less fortunate. Use your change of circumstance for the best. What good can you do? And, just maybe, that would be better than this revenge you seek."

Lamia froze and looked at her, colour warming her cheeks. Theodora smiled, a soft, knowing smile.

"You miss out on the best of things life has to offer when you pursue vengeance. Revenge does nothing but eat away at you, Your Majesty."

Lamia looked away in shame, not caring to admit that it was already her life.

"Maybe this is the second chance they would have wanted you to have? This person you seek revenge for…"

Lamia worried her lip, the thought unsettling in its veracity.

"And, you can't disagree," Theodora continued, "there are worse bed fellows to be had. I never heard any of the previous queens I served complain."

"Theodora!" Lamia exclaimed, blushing more deeply.

"Well, only of his girth!" Theodora snickered wickedly, ignoring her. "Some worried if it would fit! Here, let me help you out of the gown."

It was as she worked on the gown's fastenings that there was a knock at the door and it opened to reveal a servant bearing a tray, Hezron by their side.

"That will be the ointment. Just over there, please, Hezron," Theodora said, and Hezron directed the servant to place the tray down on the bedside table. In its centre was a small ceramic pot.

Ushering the servant out, Hezron followed, closing the door behind him as he took up his post outside the chamber once more.

"What's so special about the ointment?" Lamia asked, curiosity getting the better of her as she eyed the inconspicuous pot.

She stepped out of the gown and Theodora hung it up, smoothing down the skirts. Walking over to the tray in her stay, Lamia picked up the ceramic pot, removing the lid to sniff the pale pink ointment inside. There were floral undertones, and it smelt wonderful, like trapped starlight on a summer's eve.

"What is it made from?" she inquired, taking in its aroma again.

"I'm not entirely sure. All I know is it's fantastic for healing cuts and bruises. His Excellency has many special plants and trees in his collection, some of which only the Healers have access to. This is made from one of them. It's an ointment that the Healers use in their care of the Blood Sacrifices. We'll apply it after your bath. Come now, before the water gets cold."

"IT'S BEAUTIFUL!" LAMIA breathed.

Having washed away her tears and the dirt from the day, Lamia felt a lot better. Theodora's words weighed on her and she mulled over them as she soaked in the warm waters. She hadn't yet stopped bathing when Hezron opened the doors. The seamstress and her attendants came in carrying a resplendent silk gown in a gold which shimmered like liquid sunlight.

Lamia gasped, sitting up in wonder. "By the gods, it's beautiful!"

The seamstress hid her beaming smile with difficulty and quickly bobbed a curtsy. "Thank you, Your Majesty. His Excellency was most particular about its design."

"He was?" Lamia said, stepping out of the bath as Theodora wrapped her with a towel.

"Oh, yes. He has a fine eye."

Going over to it, Lamia held out a tentative hand to the glistening material. "I've never seen anything so beautiful."

"Wait until you see it on!" Theodora enthused.

The seamstress turned to go.

"Please wait for me outside. I should love you to be the first to see it," Lamia said.

The seamstress looked suddenly overwhelmed, and tears filled her eyes. "Thank you, Your Majesty. You're too kind."

With an approving smile, Theodora nodded to Hezron, who held the door open as they left.

She turned to Lamia with a flourish. "Let's make you into a Queen!"

THEODORA HELPED HER into the golden gown. Its silk slid over her, fitting her like a second skin. The material was momentarily cool against her and reminded her of the Emperor's touch. Its skirts puddling behind her, and its notched cap sleeves accentuated the gentle curve of her shoulders. Exposed, her burn lay bare for all to see. Its sore, blotched skin in contrast to the smooth skin of her arms.

Theodora lifted the pot of cream. "Before I forget." And she opened it. Released, its sweet fragrance wafted over them. She breathed it in with her eyes closed. "Beautiful." Taking a small amount on a fingertip, she gently dabbed it onto the wound. And waited.

Lamia glanced up at her watchful eyes with scepticism. "Really?"

An excited look passed over the girl's eyes and Lamia looked down to see the pink of the cream shimmer and sparkle like starlight, settling on her until it seeped into the wound. Lamia gasped to see the blisters shimmer and melt away into clear, unblemished skin. She held up her wrist, eyes wide. She realised she was trembling.

"It's... It's gone!"

"I know! Isn't it marvellous?" Theodora gushed, closing the pot once more. "That's going to confuse the hell out of Lady Visha!"

Lamia inhaled sharply. "Oh, no!"

Theodora placed a fist on her hip. "Well, would you rather face his wrath or hers? I know which one I would choose!"

She had a point.

Applying makeup, she complimented the look with a wash of gold over her eyelids before taking a step back to admire her handiwork. She gave a curt nod of approval and spritzed her with perfume. Lamia let her hands smooth over the skirts, hand stitched with such care and skill, and smiled.

"How do you feel?"

Lamia admired her reflection, resplendent in the golden gown. "Totally different," she admitted.

"And, now, the finishing touch," said Theodora, standing on a stool to fit a headpiece within her curls. It had spokes of gold that splintered the space above her like rays of sunlight.

"Perfect," the Fæ girl repeated. "You are the sun to his night. There is no better union."

LAMIA EMERGED FROM her chambers to excited chatter, which immediately changed to gasps and squeals of awe. She gave a shy twirl and met the seamstress's eyes, who was shaking her head in wonder.

"It's beautiful, thank you!" she effused.

The seamstress clasped her hands together and was grinning from ear to ear, tears brimming her eyes. "No, *you* are beautiful. Thank you for such an honour, Your Majesty."

Bobbing a curtsy, the seamstress's attendants followed suit, each curtsying low. Moved, Lamia bowed her head in thanks and allowed herself to be led away by Hezron and Theodora.

"The Throne Room is this way, Your Majesty."

LED DOWN COUNTLESS corridors, Lamia was relieved to see that she recognised some of them from her tour earlier. Turning a corner, she found herself in an Outer Chamber that she hadn't seen before and slowed to take in her surroundings. It was decorated with portraits of Myrrithia's many kingdoms and their palaces. There was a landscape painting of Noxterra's mountains, their peaks reaching high into an amethyst sky. The Eternal Palace glowing in the sunset. There were paintings of the lush forests of Elphyne and the palaces of the Winter and Summer Courts; the twisty mountains of Draakonia, its skies full of its famous dragon riders; as well as Shangri-La's domed palace with its many minarets. One painting showed the grassy plains of Valhalla and, in the distance, the hall of King Odin. In another, she beheld the grand underwater palace of Atlantis with its glistening corals. Whilst another portrayed a glorious cloudscape with gold staining their billowing masses from the setting sun. And there, amidst the cumulus clouds, was the flying island of Laputa, its white palace towering above the city from which it grew.

It was then that her eyes fell on him: Amias. He was waiting for her outside the Throne Room, by a set of doors decorated with an intricately carved gilt doorframe. The carvings were of a luscious climbing rose, winding its way up and across the doorframe on thorny briars. The workmanship was exquisite. But it was nothing to his cold beauty.

Amias had changed also, into a simple tunic of black with gold detailing that emphasised his height and lean muscles. His dark hair was loose over his shoulders. Though he didn't wear his cloak of raven feathers, he wore a simple gold crown. A dark look clouded his eyes, which were fixed on her approach. His three Felidaeon sat nearby, tails twitching.

She neared him shyly, feeling his eyes rove over her, stopping at where the burn had been on her wrist. She was startled to see his look soften almost instantly on seeing it gone, and felt her insides warm.

Arriving before him, she bent into a low curtsy. "My Lord."

Standing once more, he reached for her hand to examine the healed skin. He nodded approvingly, relief washing over him, scattering his dark look. But not completely. "My Queen."

The simple greeting sent involuntary flutters through her chest. Only to have them quashed by grief. She looked away, but Theodora's words from earlier echoed back at her. Then, mind made up, she took a deep breath and let her eyes meet his once more. She smiled shyly back at him.

He looked surprised. A hint of colour rose in his pale cheeks as he hesitated, seemingly unsure what to do next.

Lamia waited expectantly, feeling his hand still in hers.

Theodora gave a light cough from where she and Hezron waited at a polite distance. The Emperor looked over at them in surprise, as if noticing them for the first time. Clearing his throat, he offered an elbow to Lamia. She took it.

"Now," he said, taking a deep breath as if to steady nerves, "let us officially introduce you to my court." He motioned to the footmen on either side of the door. With a whistle, the three Felidaeon got to their feet, bending their backs in leisurely stretches before joining them, flanking them like guards.

Inhaling, she was suddenly overcome with a heady mix of nerves and excitement.

As the doors slowly opened, she felt him squeeze her hand and caught his eye in surprise.

He leaned close and Lamia caught the wild scents of his perfume. It smelt earthy, of pine needles and wild spices. Lowering his voice so only she could hear, he said, "My Queen. You look utterly divine. More radiant and beautiful than the sun itself."

With the doors cast wide, they stepped out into the Throne Room. But her eyes saw him and only him.

8

My Queen

The entire Court of the Eternal Palace had gathered in their finery to welcome their new queen.

Nothing could have prepared her for the crowds waiting in the room. The doors opened, and the chatter immediately stopped. All heads turned excitedly in their direction, parting to create an aisle. And, at its end, a dais with two thrones.

It was a grand room carved from the same black stone that made up the exterior of the Eternal Palace. Enchanted lights in sconces illuminated the hall's vaulted ceiling, igniting the stone's natural colours of purple and blue. Setting its veins of gold afire as they passed down the aisle. Amias walked with all the dignity of the Emperor he was, meeting the eyes of his courtiers whilst maintaining an other-worldly grace, whereas Lamia found herself fumbling. Either catching her footing in the skirts of her gown or shying away from so many eyes fixed on her. One of the Felidaeon butted her leg reassuringly, walking closer as if hoping to offer some sort of protection.

The Court was made up of people from some of Noxterra's most prestigious houses. Not to mention, guests from further afield—Fæ from the Unseelie Court, unicorn lords and wolf shifters from Khandûrn, merlords from Atlantis, rajas from Shangri-la, dragon riders from Draakonia, ice warriors from Calahearn, Magai representatives from Sgoil Draoidheachd, the school of magic, and angel knights from Laputa.

Guided down a central aisle through the crowd of finely dressed men and women, Lamia noticed the hum of murmurs following in their wake. They approached the dais and Amias led her up its steps to one of the two thrones upon it. Stopping her before one throne, he took up his place in front of the other. The Felidaeon stepped on to the dais, settling around his throne, though the one that had walked with Lamia chose to sit beside her.

Turning, the Emperor faced his courtiers. "Thank you so much for coming together to welcome my new bride. It is my utmost pleasure to present Lamia Fontaine, the new Queen of Forever! My new consort. My Queen!"

He took her hand and flung it up high. As one, the court bowed to the chants of 'Hail! Queen of Forever!'

She looked out over the chanting crowds as if seeing it from someone else's point of view. It was the most surreal thing she'd experienced. Well, second to his death...

A wave of guilt and grief threatened to overwhelm her, but she caught Theodora looking at her from where she stood with Hezron at the back of the hall, and her words echoed back to her. *What good can you do?*

He would want her to do good, wouldn't he?

Sudden quiet tore her from her turmoil and she found Amias smiling proudly across at her. It was the most beautiful thing she'd ever seen. Before she could register the twist of her heart, he gestured for her to sit. Arranging her skirts, she sat as he turned to address his court once more.

"It is time for you to pledge your loyalty to your Queen." His demeanour suddenly changed, darkening before them. It seemed as if the shadows themselves had come alive. When he next spoke, his voice was like the edge of a blade: sharp and deadly. "The Queen is not only your Queen, but she is also *my* Queen. *Mine.* And, if there is *ever* any transgression against her, you shall forfeit with your life. It shall not be quick. And I shall not be merciful."

The stunned silence that followed was deafening. Its weight was profound as the courtiers glanced at one another warily. Lamia stared at him in astonishment. He took the chair beside her and gestured to the Herald. Leaping into action, they made their first announcement.

"The Queen's Father, Miklaus Fontaine, and the Queen's Mother, Delilah Fontaine!"

Lamia strained her neck to see her parents appear from the front of the crowds. She couldn't help the smile on seeing them both. They were both dressed in the finest of clothes—it looked like her mother may have convinced her father to indulge in some shopping on learning of their introduction to the Emperor's court! As Miklaus and Delilah were led down the aisle, Lamia couldn't help but get to her feet. Amias joined her, and they walked down the steps of the dais together. On arriving, her parents bowed and curtsied low. When they rose, Amias embraced them warmly, kissing their cheeks as he murmured his welcome. Stunned, her parents looked at each other excitedly before Lamia threw her arms around them.

"Darling!" her mother cried, kissing her fondly. "You look exquisite!"

"Thank you."

A steward hovered beside them, and Delilah reluctantly let go of her daughter.

Before they left, Amias took their hands. "You are welcome to stay as long as you wish. I have had a suite prepared for you."

Miklaus and Delilah stammered their thanks as they bowed and curtsied once more.

He waved them away. "Honestly, there is no need. You are family now."

He gestured, and Theodora appeared like magic. "Before they enjoy the celebrations, please show the Queen's parents to the Queen's suite. Make arrangements for their belongings to be transferred there."

Theodora curtsied. "As you wish, Your Excellency. Please, follow me."

Watching them leave via a side door, Lamia was guided back up the steps to the throne by Amias, who only sat once she was comfortably settled. The Herald began their introductions, announcing princes and princesses, counts and countesses, lords and ladies from all four corners of Myrrithia. There were representatives from all of Myrrithia's kingdoms. With their names announced, they approached the dais to bow and curtsy before them, pledging their loyalty. Following Amias' lead, Lamia nodded her thanks to each, smiling demurely. At first, she was determined to learn each name and face, but there were so many. They passed by in a blur. Countless faces and names that she had no hope of remembering. Pledges made, she noticed them shown out via a set of double doors. Each time they opened, laughter and music spilled out. A party!

"Do not look so forlorn, My Queen," said a voice beside her.

She jumped to find Amias kneeling beside her throne.

Had she been so obvious?!

"This is nothing," he said, waving a dismissive hand at the double doors. He took her hand in his and leaned close with a conspiratorial air. "I am hosting an even bigger ball in your honour tomorrow night."

"You are?" she stammered, eyes wide.

He nodded.

Just then, the Herald's voice rang out clear. "King Morozko of the Unseelie Court and his sons, Prince Aquilo and Prince Boreas."

Amias whirled round, smiling to see the new arrivals. Three men stood together, one older than the other two. The older man had black hair and wore an imperial crown like that which Amias wore, though his had a gem of the palest blue at its centre. He shared a vague resemblance to the Emperor, with the same haughty brow and high cheekbones. Though his eyes were a pale blue and not violet.

"Morozko!" Amias cried, rushing to fling his arms around the older man with affection. The two men embraced. "This is my great-nephew on my late elder brother's side," he explained.

Lamia gave a graceful curtsy. "It is a pleasure to make your acquaintance, Your Majesty."

"The pleasure is all mine, Your Majesty," Morozko replied, bowing deeply. "Please allow me to introduce my sons, Prince Aquilo and Prince Boreas."

Despite the similar strong lines of their jaws and their matching pale blue eyes, the two brothers were, on appearances, as different as they could ever be. The eldest had long black hair like their father, though flecked with the occasional errant white strand. Whilst his younger brother had hair of the starkest white, which he wore cropped short except for one braid plaited and tied off with a brown leather cord.

There was a stiffness to Aquilo's shoulders, which transferred to his bow, unlike Boreas, who bowed with graceful ease. When Boreas looked up at her, Lamia couldn't help but smile to see the mischievous twinkle there. It was then she stopped short, double taking to see their snowflake-shaped irises. Realising her rudeness, she quickly curtsied back.

The Herald coughed again. There was a queue of courtiers waiting.

Morozko and Amias shared a look.

"Duty calls," Amias said apologetically.

Morozko waved his hand dismissively. "We still have time on our side. We are here a few days more, My Lord."

"Wonderful. I look forward to seeing you tomorrow, nephew."

And, with that, the men left via the double doors.

Returning to their seats, time seemed to lose all meaning as names were introduced and face after face greeted them. Whenever she looked to see who remained, the queue seemed to trail on forever. She sighed. It was then she noticed the enchanted lights igniting the lustrous gold of her gown. Marvelling at its depth, she couldn't help but wonder if the material had indeed been spun from the famous gold thread from the Goldspinner legends. Feeling herself tire, she was about to request a drink when a glass appeared on a tray.

"You looked as if you could do with a 'pick-me-up'," the Emperor said, nodding his thanks to the servant.

Thanking the servant herself, she took a sip. It was light and cold and fizzed with a concoction of sweet fruity flavours. Before she knew it, she'd gulped it all down and was wishing for more.

"Lord Vasilis and his wife, Lady Elyssia," the Herald's voice said.

Lamia looked up to find Amias standing, a look of delight on his face as his eyes fell on the couple before the dais.

The man was tall, with long grey-white hair and steely grey eyes. In the centre of his forehead was a pale tattoo of a star. His aloof air softened on seeing Amias quickly dismount the steps to take his hand. In contrast, the Fæ lady at his side had chestnut hair and dazzling green eyes that sparked with intelligence and shrewdness. A pair of glistening fairy wings adorned her back.

"You sly dog!" Amias said, shaking his hand. "I was unaware you had wed!"

Vasilis blushed, glancing over at his wife. "Sorry, I would have sent you an invitation, dear friend, but it took me by surprise, too."

Elyssia flashed her husband a secretive smile.

"You said Eldermoor was boring with little to offer proper society, yet here you bring the most enchanting of wives!" Amias took Elyssia's hand in his and placed a kiss on its back.

"Oh, he did, did he, Your Excellency?" Elyssia said.

"That was before everything," Vasilis argued, catching her eye. "Before I fell in love with you."

Elyssia regarded him, a playful glint in her green eyes. "It had better be."

Lamia felt a stab of jealousy as she walked down the steps of the dais to join Amias, wishing that she had such a close marriage.

Seeing her, Vasilis gave a gallant bow and Elyssia curtsied.

"Vasilis is a good friend of mine. Despite what people say of unicorns and vampires, we get along well."

Unicorn?

Lamia gaped. "I've never met a Unicorn Lord!"

"Oh, do not feed his ego, please, Your Majesty. It is far too big already!" Elyssia moaned. "He was a pompous idiot when I first met him, and I have no wish to revisit that version of himself."

"You didn't get along?"

"By the gods, no! I hated him! He was a prick," she laughed, casting him a sideways look of adoration.

Lamia blinked.

Elyssia caught her eye and laughed again. "I'll happily tell you our chaotic tale another time, Your Majesty."

"I look forward to it."

There was a cough as the Herald cleared his throat.

"That's our cue!" Elyssia grinned. "See you anon, Your Majesty. Oh, and I'd be careful of that one," she said, eyes turning pointedly to who waited behind her. "She has a tongue sharper than a viper!"

Looking, Lamia saw Lady Visha waiting at the front of the queue. She was dressed in a beautiful gown of blue silk, but there was a sickly pallor to her well-made face. She was staring at Lamia's wrist where the wound had been with a look of shock.

"Though something has ruffled her," Elyssia said, interest piqued. "I look forward to speaking with you again, Your Majesty," she said, curtsying, before taking her husband's hand and exiting via the double doors.

Lamia watched her leave reluctantly.

"Making friends I see?"

"She was nice."

"Yes, he chose well. Lady Elyssia is exactly the sort of bride he needs. I am curious to hear their tale. He always vowed never to marry."

Lamia had the sudden urge to ask if she was the sort of bride he needed when the Herald gestured for her to return to her throne. Chiding herself for such silly thoughts, she adjusted her skirts and prepared to face Lady Visha.

"Lady Visha of Dunbarrow!" the Herald announced.

Gathering her composure, Lady Visha floated gracefully to the floor in a deep curtsy.

"Thank you for looking after my Queen this morning," Amias said, once she had pledged her loyalty to the Queen.

"Not at all, My Lord. You know I'm always happy to help."

He sat with an apparent lazy air upon his throne, his legs crossed. He leaned forward, eyes darkening. "Then, maybe you can shed some light on an injury my Queen sustained this morning."

"An injury, My Lord?" She rose innocent blue eyes to his. "It must have happened once we'd parted ways."

Lamia felt his gaze rove over to her and she kept her face as impassive as possible.

"I suppose it must have," he said, his tone soft and deadly. "Well, I'm sure the person is aware of the danger they are in if such a transgression happens again."

"Yes, I am sure they are," Lady Visha said.

Lamia couldn't help but marvel at her level tone.

With a final curtsy, Lady Visha left without a backward glance. It was only as she exhaled that Lamia realised she'd been holding her breath. Forcing a smile, she faced the last few members of the court. After what seemed like hours, the final courtiers had introduced themselves and exited to join the others through the side doors.

"You comported yourself marvellously, My Queen!" Amias said with appreciation. "It is a tiresome but necessary introduction to court. I need them to know where they stand."

Lamia was about to comment that everyone now knew exactly where they stood after his speech when a servant rushed in from a side door. They looked up in surprise. It was a Healer. The lady was dressed all in white: a white dress with a matching white headdress and apron. Blood splatters marred its pureness. A look of absolute distress marred her pretty face.

"Your Excellency! It's Ward 87158!"

"Felicity? The child?" Amias said, leaping to his feet. He rushed over to the lady. "What's happened?"

"A turn for the worse, I'm afraid, Your Excellency."

Amias turned to Lamia, and something she hadn't seen before was in his eyes: dread. He hesitated then, as if he might come over to her, but stopped himself at the last second. He licked his lips, eyes meeting hers.

"I-I'm afraid I must leave, My Queen. Please excuse me."

Lamia nodded numbly. "Of course, My Lord."

Sensing his agitation, the Felidaeon rose, padding over to him.

Theodora and Hezron appeared then, having rushed over from the end of the Throne Room. "We shall look after her, Your Excellency."

"Thank you," he said, smiling in appreciation at them. He turned to Lamia, still hesitant. "Do not wait up. I could be some time. I'm sorry."

Before she could reply, he was gone.

Lamia stared at where he had been for longer than was necessary.

"Your Majesty?" Theodora asked tentatively. "Is everything alright?"

Admonishing herself, Lamia turned to leave. "Yes, thank you. Please, may I have some refreshment in my rooms? I'm suddenly feeling quite tired."

"Certainly, Your Majesty."

9

Summoned

Lamia woke from her bundles of blankets on the settee to find the bed empty. Its covers undisturbed, as if Amias hadn't slept in it that night.

She sat up, feeling dazed.

What could have kept him all night?

There was a knock at the door and it opened to reveal Theodora's head poking round. A look of confusion washed over her when she saw the empty bed. Scanning the room. Her eyes finally rested on Lamia's curled up form and gave a half-smile.

"Sleep well, Your Majesty?"

Lamia shrugged bashfully. "So-so. Do you know where the Emperor is? I don't think he slept here last night."

"No, he was... preoccupied. He's currently greeting new Blood Sacrifices," she said, entering and crossing straight over to the bathtub.

Lamia stilled. "New Blood Sacrifices?" Her voice sounded tight even to her ears.

"Yes, once admitted, they are referred to as 'wards,'" she explained over the sound of running water. "The Emperor welcomes them in person to the palace every Chapel Day with the High Priest. He usually then gives them a personal tour of the Hospital Wing."

"He has servants. Why would he do it himself?"

"It is something he is quite particular about, Your Majesty. He is very protective of his Wards."

Lamia found that hard to believe.

Theodora crossed over to the armoire and fetched out a pretty stay and chemise before selecting a stunning gown in dark blue silk. "Time to get ready, Your Majesty."

STANDING BEFORE THE mirror whilst Theodora put the finishing touches to her hair, Lamia admired the blue of the gown. Somehow it matched her eyes perfectly, setting them aglow. Trimmed with intricate gold silk, the gown featured a scalloped neckline and notched cap sleeves to emphasise her slender neck.

Spritzing some perfume, Theodora stood back with a smile. "He won't be able to keep his hands off you!"

Before Lamia could say anything, there was a knock at the door and Hezron appeared with Rûntal. A large Felidaeon was at his heels, its whiskers twitching as it sniffed the perfumed air.

Theodora flashed Lamia a triumphant look.

"Yes?" Theodora asked.

Remembering himself, the knight bowed. "His Excellency wonders if the Queen would do him the honour of joining him for lunch."

Lamia froze, eyes widening as they met Theodora's hazel ones.

"Her Majesty would be delighted," Theodora said for her.

"B-but I was hoping to have lunch with my parents," Lamia began.

Rûntal cleared his throat. "I'm afraid your parents are, erm, feeling rather tender from last night's gathering, Your Majesty."

Lamia sighed.

Typical. Her mother always got carried away when there was champagne.

Theodora finished fastening a choker, letting its drooping pendant adorn her collarbone, and flashed Lamia a sultry smile.

"Perfect."

LAMIA FINALLY FOUND herself admitted to a cosy study. Its walls were lined with floor-to-ceiling bookcases filled with leather-bound tomes, whilst its windows overlooked the palace gardens with its flower beds, walkways and sculpted topiary. The tops of an orchard could be seen in the distance. A fire had been lit and close by was a desk and two chairs. Behind the desk sat the Emperor smoking a dainty black pipe. Rose coloured smoke wafted through the air. It smelt pleasant.

A hint of anger thrummed through her at the sight of him, but with Theodora's wise counsel, it was less consuming. She even found herself glad to see him well after last night's sudden disappearance.

He put down his paperwork as she was announced and eyed her with greedy appreciation.

"My Lord," Lamia said, curtsying low.

He rose and walked round the desk to her. He wore a dark blue tunic, a long jacket of silver brocade, tight-fitted black breeches, and a pair of black leather boots. His long hair was loose over his shoulders. Instead of his crown, he wore a modest diadem atop his brow. Stopping barely a foot from her, she could see the dark shadows under his eyes and just how soft his lips were.

"Greetings, My Queen. I see Theodora has been looking after you. The gown becomes you as I thought it might," he said, eyes drifting to the pendant that rested against her chest.

"Yes, My Lord. She has been most attentive."

"Only the best for you, My Queen. I trust you slept well?"

"I did, My Lord, thank you."

He smiled, showing the tips of his fangs, before returning to consider her, puffing contentedly on his pipe. The Felidaeon, having grown weary of waiting next to the Guard, entered, padding over to the Emperor to nuzzle against his hand. He stroked the animal absentmindedly as he regarded her.

"Is this your library?" Lamia asked, seeking ways to fill the unnerving quiet.

"Hmm?" He roused himself from his reverie to catch her eye. "Library? No, this is my study. I hold court every weekday until mid-morn, then I attend to paperwork and the palace until night. Chapel Day is spent with my Wards and catching up with paperwork ready for the new week. When I'm alone, that is." He unpacked his pipe, knocking it clean.

"And when you're not alone?"

"I seek greater... *diversions*. Have you eaten?"

"No, My Lord."

"Excellent! Rûntal," he said, turning to his son who stood guard by the door, "please arrange for us to eat in the Library. I shall escort the Queen," the Emperor said, pocketing his pipe before offering his arm to Lamia.

"Yes, father," Rûntal said. "Heel Vayr." And the Felidaeon traipsed over with a lazy swagger. Bowing, the guard and big cat left.

Wrapping her hand firmly around his arm, Amias led her down the hall before she could protest. Lamia was acutely aware that her mother would admonish her greatly for her previous treatment of the Emperor when she found out, so tried her best to behave. She soon found herself distracted by his lively tales of the palace and its Music Room, Picture Gallery, Drawing Room, Throne Room, and Central Court. All the while, Hezron followed at a respectful distance, keeping watch.

Many of the rooms she was now familiar with, but despite herself, she gazed round the Central Court in amazement. Having not been admitted the other morning, she hadn't been able to appreciate its magnificence. Her father had once visited the Court Room with some colleagues to have a case heard by the Emperor and his advisors. He had always talked of the experience with fondness. Lamia was thrilled to see that his descriptions of the lavish Central Court were not unfounded. Unlike the palace, the Central Court was made of stone. With its ribbed vaulting and wide columns decorated in geometric patterns, it was quite breathtaking.

Amias watched her turn to take in its beauty. "You like it?"

"My father came here to have a case heard... I always thought he was exaggerating how beautiful it was!" she gushed, unable to contain herself.

"He did?" The Emperor looked intrigued. "I hope I heard his case well."

"Yes, he said you were cold, but fair."

The Emperor seemed to consider this for a moment before reaching for her hand to lead her through a side door. "Let me show you one of my favourite rooms."

He caught Hezron's eye and winked.

10

The Library

Leading her down one particular corridor, he opened a set of double doors to reveal a vaulted library split across several floors. Spiral stairs led off to the upper levels, whilst Noxterra's tepid daylight filtered down from a glass dome in the roof. The shelves were filled with books of all shapes and sizes, whilst more curios from all four corners of Myrrithia lay dotted around.

Lamia could barely contain her excitement. "This is all yours?! I've seen nothing so wonderful! I always thought the library in Gerran was fine, but it's nothing compared to this! You even have ladders!" She exclaimed, darting for the nearest set of rolling ladders, and climbed the first couple of rungs eagerly.

"What is a library if it has no ladders?" Amias said, smiling at her delight.

"Every Queen loves the library," Hezron said, with a wistful smile. "Mother was the same."

The table by the fire had been set for two. A fire burned merrily in the grate and in front, basking in its heat, lay the other two Felidaeon.

Amias smiled at his son. "It certainly goes in my favour."

"Ah, but is your collection on dull history and politics, or on adventures and mystery?" she asked.

Amias joined her as she reached for a book. "Well, in my experience, history is only dull if it is told poorly, but, I admit, my collection of fiction far outweighs my collection of non." His eyes twinkled, softening his cool demeanour.

At that moment, Rûntal appeared with Vayr at his side, leading servants bearing trays of food. The Felidaeon padded over to join its companions before the fire.

"Do you require anything more, father?" Rûntal asked as he checked everything was in order. Amias wandered over to his two sons.

"No disturbances, please. You never know, I might have more luck today."

Rûntal patted his father on his shoulder. "It can't get any worse."

"I sincerely hope not," Amias said, glancing over his shoulder at Lamia, who still stood with her nose in the book.

Lamia was too busy flicking through the book in her hands to even realise the servants, and Hezron and Rûntal had left. It was only when Amias placed a hand on either side of the ladder, bracing himself just against her, that she lowered the book. Her eyes widened to find them alone.

"Does it take your fancy?" The Emperor asked from over her shoulder.

"It's sadly politics," she said, ignoring the sudden thunder of her heart.

He pulled a face. "Certainly not the most enthralling. Let's see..."

With a jerk, he set the ladder in motion, rolling it to the right. Losing her balance, Lamia instinctively reached behind her to steady herself, only to find her grasping his thigh. She let out a nervous laugh as she quickly placed her hand on the ladder.

Amias cleared his throat and turned his attention to the bookcases. "Tales of Myrrithia. Myths and Legends. Farming and agriculture. Gardening and Herbology," he said, reeling off the books as they passed.

"Herbology?"

Seeing her interest piqued, he brought the ladder to a stop in front of the herbology section.

"Thank you," she said, turning shyly to peruse the shelves. It was quite a collection!

"Any knives hidden in your garter today?" he asked, after a moment's quiet.

She glanced over her shoulder at him. His eyes were roaming over her curves, accentuated by the cut of the gown. "No, I'm not wearing one today."

"Shame."

"Anyway, you confiscated the letter opener and broke my knife." She returned her attention to the books, selecting one.

"Perhaps in your stay?"

She raised a brow at him. "I thought you said I was cliché?"

"I said the knives were getting cliché, not you," he said, joining her on her rung of the ladder, so he virtually embraced her. "You are *far* from cliché. But, on reflection, the thought is quite arousing."

"That I might kill you at any minute?" she asked over her shoulder.

"That you might care enough to, yes. That you might have something sharp waiting for me here..." His hand roamed up her thigh, getting dangerously close.

It was unexpectedly delicious.

She inhaled sharply against the thought and shivered.

"Let me warm you," he said, mistaking her trembles as those caused by the cold. Lifting her hair to scatter kisses along the curves of her shoulder, burning their way to the crook of her neck.

Despite herself, she marvelled at the shivers his kisses sent through her and wanted more. Offering him her neck, she gasped as he took the invitation, leaving a whisper of kisses up her exposed throat to suck and kiss near her ear. His fangs grazed her skin—who thought it could be so heavenly?!

He let a hand venture along the swell of her hip and backside to linger on the small of her exposed back, all the way to shadow along the wings of her shoulder blades. She tremored in anticipation and moaned to hear his breath in her ears, to feel his hips pinning her in place, to feel the hardness of the ladder behind her. Imprisoning her. The thought was as nerve-racking as it was arousing.

"This gown is most exquisite on you," he murmured, voice honey-smooth.

"Thank you," she stammered, hardly able to think straight because of the waves of desire pulsing through her.

She needed a knife, didn't she?

In a daze, her grip of the book loosened, and it slipped from her hand. The *thud!* of it meeting the floor startling her out of her bliss.

"Leave it," he pleaded, kissing her neck once more, letting them trickle all the way to the edges of her lips.

They brushed hers, as soft as she'd imagined, and she inhaled in anticipation.

Seizing the opportunity, he turned her to face him. The glow of his purple eyes haunting as they took her in. Before she could shy away, a hand appeared to tuck a curl behind her ear. He let it caress the side of her face, from the temple to her jaw, tilting her chin to carefully, cautiously, kiss her.

Eyes closed against the sensation, she marvelled at how gentle he was. Until The Picking she hadn't dreamt of being kissed by the Emperor, but to say it hadn't featured in her dreams since would've been a lie. Thankfully, they didn't disappoint. If she wasn't aware he was kissing her, she would have thought a butterfly had landed on her, its wings brushing gently against her.

Teasing her, tracing the outline of her lips with his tongue, she found herself opening her mouth to him. Inviting him in against her better judgement. And he came, kissing her with all the adoration of a believer at Chapel. Kissing her with slow, languid kisses of reverence.

He cupped her neck, deepening the kiss as his tongue explored her. And she let him. Even daring to explore him herself.

He gasped in pleasant surprise, clutching her hip to bring her close against his hardness.

She thought she knew kissing, thought she knew, but she didn't. Not until now.

The heat that exploded within her, making her breath come short and her head spin, was like none other. She kept trying to remember why she had been angry at him. Why she would never stop being angry at him... Could never stop... But, as he undid her with each kiss, she found the rage abating until all she thought of was him.

"No..." she gasped. "No, I can't..."

"I'll stop if you want me to," he said, in between kisses, "but I don't think you do..."

He caught her eye, saw her hesitation and smiled sultrily, fangs visible. With one hand braced against the ladder, he let his other trail from her neck, along her collarbone and down the centre of her chest to the rise and fall of her breast. Tenderly stroking its crown, he tugged away the neckline, letting the dress slip off her shoulder to expose her chemise and stay. She felt heat rising in her cheeks.

This was the most exposed she'd ever been in front of a man. But she knew it would only increase. Acutely aware that she'd denied her husband—the Emperor of all Noxterra, no less—the intimacy of her company, she knew she would have to let him. Though, if it continued like this, it would definitely be more of a pleasure than a chore.

"You're wearing them?" he whispered. A soft smile lightened his face. "I picked them out just for you."

But before she could say anything, she welcomed another kiss as he eased her out of the stay, revealing a nipple. Heart hammering against her chest, she felt him take the nipple between his fingers and gently tease it before placing it in his mouth. Gasping at the new sensation, she felt herself groaning from the feel of his tongue sucking and flicking over its peak. She covered her mouth from shyness, cheeks reddening even more.

"No, don't," he said, catching her hand in his. "Moan and groan all you like." He kissed her neck. "It is the sweetest of music. They fuel my fire for you..."

And he bent to pull down the material covering her other breast.

"They're a good handful," he said, smiling down at her whilst idly fondling them.

"Are they?" she breathed, surprising herself at her flirty tone.

"Extremely," he said, lips meeting hers as he lifted a thigh to wrap around his waist.

Running his hand under her skirts, he marvelled at her skin, smooth and supple, relishing the feel of her bum as he squeezed it. He pressed his arousal against her, and she inhaled to feel its throbbing hardness straining through his breeches. Her mind skipped automatically to the sneak preview granted on their wedding night. A great heat arose in her groin, overwhelming her.

"Do you feel that?" he whispered hoarsely. "That's what you do to me, Lamia. And it's all for you."

"All of it?" she teased.

Why was she teasing him?

"Every last inch," he breathed. "And that's a lot. You remember our wedding night?"

She nodded, biting her lower lip as he swayed against her, bringing their hips closer together.

"You want to do this here, Amias?" she asked, hands coasting over his chest to brush the hair from his face. It was soft and trickled through her fingers like fine silk. She'd been longing to feel it.

He paused at the sound of his name on her lips, the feel of her hands raking through his hair, and a warm glow set his eyes afire. Then, lips quirking in a saucy smile, he braced himself on either side of her, leaning so close his hair fell like a dark curtain around them. "I would *do* you anywhere and everywhere. I would fill the halls with your cries."

As his lips met hers with increased urgency, there was a knock at the door. He glared at it with such vexation Lamia almost laughed.

They waited, eyeing each other.

Perhaps the person had thought better of it?

She made to amend her gown. "Maybe we should—"

"You're not going anywhere," he growled, leaning to wrap his fingers around her throat.

He leaned forward to take her lips with his.

Another knock sounded, and he cursed.

"I said no disturbances!" he barked, storming to the door.

It was Rûntal. He looked worried.

"Sorry father, I wouldn't have disturbed you but—"

"But *what?*" Amias asked, not even trying to mask his exasperation.

"It's the ward, father."

Amias froze and Lamia looked over with interest as she straightened her bodice and skirts.

Amias pinched the bridge of his nose. When he spoke, his voice was as heavy as the mountains that circled Dårath. "Felicity?"

Rûntal nodded sadly. "The Healers are with her now. They are moving her to a private suite."

"I see. Please keep me posted." Amias' shoulders drooped as he sighed.

"Of course, father," Rûntal said, peering round to spy a flustered-looking Lamia. "Sorry for disturbing you."

Amias waved his hand dismissively. "As I said, keep me posted. If they require more petals, let them."

Rûntal bowed and closed the doors behind him.

At first, Amias stood facing the closed door, leaning against it heavily, his head bowed. When he turned back to her, he looked older and wearier. "Sorry, My Queen. Some matters of state. Shall we take some lunch?"

Gesturing to the table, he pulled back the chair nearest the fire for her, tucking her in once she was ready. Only then did he take the seat opposite. She helped herself to a selection of cheeses and meats with homemade bread as he prepared his pipe, adding a helping of red-coloured tobacco. Once packed, he lit it, settling back to observe her, his weariness slowly ebbing as he puffed on the pipe. Noone had ever looked at her with such interest. She felt quite exposed and more than a little self-conscious.

She sniffed the air. The smoke was pale pink in colour and sweet-smelling.

"I hope you don't mind if I smoke?"

Lamia shook her head. "Of course not, My Lord."

She was desperate to ask him about the ward she'd overheard Rûntal mention to him.

"I have a gift for you, My Queen."

"Tonight's ball?"

"No, another gift."

Lamia shied away. "You don't need to get me any more gifts, My Lord."

"No, I don't. But I should like to. Consider it a home warming present. I am aware settling into a new home, let alone a new life, brings with it mixed emotions."

She cut him a look as she pushed aside her plate. "You could say that."

Amias's lips curled into a smile. "Your wit is as sharp as that blade you had hid so well within your garter."

Lamia swallowed against the lump in her throat. "Thank you, My Lord."

The Emperor leaned forward, purple eyes bright, and a hand appeared on her thigh. "I was quite jealous of it. Being so close..." She watched as his hand crept slowly up her thigh, squeezing the spot where her garter had been.

Inhaling sharply as heat filled her, it took every bit of her control to not open her legs to invite him in. To see what he'd do, to feel him closer. "You could always gift me a new blade."

"You know," he began, looking up into her eyes, "I think it might just be worth the risk."

Knocking his pipe clean, he stood and offered her a hand. "Come, let me show you."

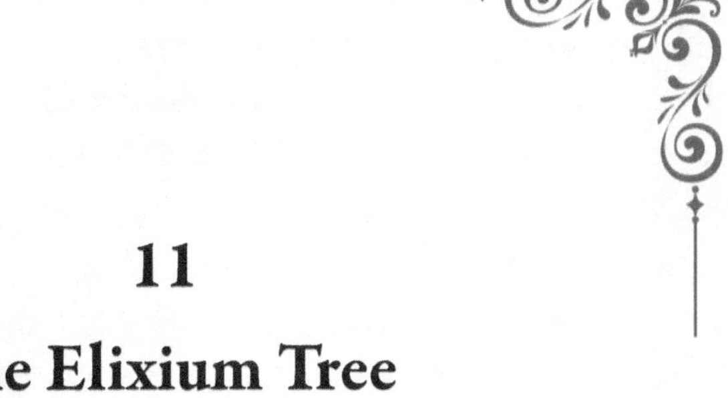

11

The Elixium Tree

The palace gardens stretched out before her. The mountain ranges amongst which the city of Dårath nestled were a bruised blue on the horizon, visible over the palace walls. Though spring in Noxterra retained a hint of winter upon its breeze, the sun remained low in the sky. Plants were sprouting in the beds that spread out over the stepped terraces, and buds were forming on the trees. A bridge curved over a channel of water where lilies grew.

Lamia looked out over the scene. Though the flowers had yet to bloom, it was still beautiful. She could almost sense the garden coming to life beneath her very feet.

"Do you like it?" he asked, leading her over the bridge. He wore a dagger from his belt, fetching it as they exited the palace and insisting to Hezron that he himself would look after the Queen.

"It... It's the most beautiful garden I've ever seen." And that was true. Whilst it was yet to bloom, she could see it in her mind's eye, and it was glorious. "It puts mine to shame..."

"Every garden has its own beauty," he countered softly. "I feel it has yet to reach its potential. Come, this way."

He eagerly led her across the bridge, the Felidaeons padding behind them, nipping at butterflies as they went. Following him, she found them in an area planted with trees, some of which towered high above them: redwoods, ash and spruce. He spoke of the trees as if they were old friends, recounting the occasions on which he'd planted them—anniversaries, births, and deaths. Lightning had struck one tree at some point during its lifetime. Whilst it still stood proud, its evergreen needles bright in the afternoon light, a large cleft tore it almost in two.

Having not picked up a shawl from the suite, Lamia was soon shivering from the cool air. Just as she was about to ask to return for a shawl, he shrugged off his jacket and placed it over her shoulders.

"I don't feel the cold as you do," he said, fingers lingering on her arms before catching her hand in his. "This way!"

He led her on through the trees and shrubbery. Rounding a rhododendron, they stumbled across a clearing with a small stone cottage in its centre. It was stout and strong, with a thatched roof, and hugged the boughs of a towering sequoia. Its trunk was at least as wide as four Felidaeons.

"It's the old Gardener's Cottage. It's abandoned now. People rarely come this far into the gardens."

"Really? How come?"

He gave her a smile that made her nerves quiver in anticipation. "It's private."

"We're almost there," he said, leading her round the back of the cottage. His excitement was almost palpable and highly contagious. She tingled in anticipation. "Unless you object, I should like to cover your eyes."

Hesitating, she nodded, permitting him to come up behind her and cover her eyes with his hands. To feel him so close sent a thrill coursing through her, setting her on tenterhooks. Laughing nervously, she stumbled forward under his guidance, holding out her hands to steady herself.

"Just a little farther," he said, voice soft within her ears.

He brought them to a stop, but he didn't remove his hands straightaway. She quivered, almost feeling his gaze rake over the curves of her neck and shoulders.

"Now. Open them," he said, his hands disappearing.

She found herself in a large cottage garden. Its flowerbeds were devoid of life apart from the weeds. And the gravel paths looked tired and woebegone.

Lamia stopped in her tracks, her expression unreadable.

"Do you like it?" Amias asked, watching her anxiously. "It's yours, if you should like it. The cottage too."

Turning to him, she felt tears burn her eyes as the familiar sensation of distemper warmed her blood. But she refused to let them fall. She licked her lips, looking over the garden once more.

"Why would you do that?" she asked finally.

He looked taken aback. "As I said, you are not a prisoner."

"I tried to kill you. Several times, in fact."

He rubbed his neck shyly. "True. But you have lost your home and your garden, and all sense of what your life was."

She couldn't move for the guilt and anger roiling within her, fighting for dominance.

She would rather him try her and condemn her to death than make her indebted to him. Yet...

Before she could find out which would win, he'd taken her hand and was showing her the small potting shed and glasshouse. It was in a poor state. But by the time they'd made a circuit of the garden, she was already planning the borders and had a mental list of important jobs to attend to first.

"This hasn't been in use for many, many years. Few of my Queens enjoyed the outdoors, but I find it quite a solace, watching beauty grow amidst the hardships of life."

Curious about these 'hardships' the Emperor had known, she caught sight of the white robes of Healers down the path at the side of the cottage. They were heading westward, crossing in front of the cottage to disappear from view.

Without waiting for the Emperor, she followed them, positive their appearance had significance.

Why would they be in this remote corner of the palace grounds?

Hadn't Amias said it was private?

She dived back into the forest. Trees surrounded her once more, their leaves scattering the sunlight on the forest floor. Ferns gave way to grasses and wildflowers, which gave way to gorse bushes and stone. With a gasp, Lamia gazed upon a large stone dome that stretched across the valley, almost like a mausoleum except it had a large hole in the centre of its domed roof. Knights guarded its arched entrance.

Making way for the Healers, the Knights crossed their halberds, blocking her way before catching the eye of someone behind her—presumably the Emperor. Removing the halberds from her path, Lamia edged forward through the entrance. The gloom was illuminated by enchanted torches, their pearlescent glow picking out the smooth stone of the walls. Before her, she could spy steps circling downwards. For some reason, the hairs on the back of her neck were raised, and she felt breathless. Steadying herself, she followed the steps round and round into an underground temple with thick columns in white marble and a rib vaulted ceiling. Within was a circular pool, too perfect to be anything but handmade. Its waters were dark and still like a mirror and, in its centre, on an island, was a tree. Sunlight poured down through a circular opening above its crown, bathing its pink blossom in the purest of light. Within its warm glow, the petals sparkled like precious stones.

The Healers were on the island where the tree grew, having stepped across using a series of steppingstones. One was up a ladder, gently plucking flowers from its branches whilst the others stood around the ladder, chanting a calming prayer as the blossom was placed within the baskets that they held aloft. Their heads bowed as they gratefully received the glowing petals.

Lamia gasped, stumbling forward in shock at the sight of the sacred tree. "An Elixium tree! You have an Elixium tree!"

She didn't need to look to know that the Emperor was directly behind her, having followed her the whole time.

"Yes, it is the reason I remain in Noxterra, and don't return home," he said, descending the steps.

Ignoring the dozen questions his response threw up, she pointed at the tree, her blue eyes blazing from the anger ignited within.

"You keep it? For yourself?!" she seethed, thinking of the good the Elixium tree could do. Its petals and bark were renowned for their healing properties. She'd tried to buy some for her brother, but they were nigh impossible to obtain. She'd even tried purchasing a seed pod, which was exceptionally rare and cost more than her father's estate thrice over. It was said they needed it to be planted in the heart of a unicorn to grow, another obstacle in her way.

She thought of the lives it could save. She thought of her brother's life that might have been saved had she had access to such a tree.

"Yes, but—"

"You're the bloody 'King of Forever'! A self-proclaimed 'God of Death'! What need do you have for an Elixium tree?"

He halted at her curse, purple gaze hardening. The softness of his lips vanishing as they settled in a cold line.

"Do you fall ill?" she growled, not allowing him a chance to reply.

He faltered then, shifting his feet. "No."

"Do you have a life-threatening illness? Are you going to die?"

He looked away, a faint colour reaching his cheeks. "No."

"Then, why, by the names of all the gods, do you have that tree?!" She was thinking of her brother, of the illness that had robbed him of his vivacity and desire to live. Of his pale clammy skin and dull eyes. Of his laboured breathing as he lay dying in bed. The tears she'd held back ran down her cheeks unchecked.

"DO YOU KNOW THE GOOD IT COULD DO?!" she roared.

She took a step back toward the water, and Amias reached for her, concern clearly painted on his face lest she fell. Quick as a flash, she yanked off his jacket from her shoulder and threw it at him, catching him off-guard. Acting on reflex, he caught it, leaving her free to take the knife from the scabbard hanging from his belt. She swung it up and was about to plunge it through his rib cage when there was a cry.

"Stop!"

Lamia froze. The blade hovered inches from Amias' chest.

The Healers had crossed from the tree's island and were standing close by, shock clearly written on their faces. Their baskets were full of the tree's blossom. A faint glow still clung to the petals.

"How dare you befoul this place with your murderous intent?! This is a sacred place! Leave at once!" said one Healer.

Her black look vanished as Lamia turned from the Healer to the knife in her hand and the sacred tree just beyond, eyes widening in shock. Then, without another word, she turned on her heel and fled up the stairs, taking them two at a time.

"Would you like me to ask for the Guards to arrest her, Your Excellency?" the Healer asked.

The Emperor watched Lamia go, his brow heavy. "No, I'll handle it."

He looked at the baskets in their hands; the pink flowers glistening within. "Are they for Felicity?"

The Healer who had spoken bowed her head sorrowfully. "Yes, for pain relief. I fear it won't be long..."

The Emperor nodded dejectedly, weary lines appearing around his eyes, cutting deep. "I shall see her before I get ready."

❦

THEODORA PUT THE LAST finishing touches to Lamia's hair and stood back to appreciate the full effect. Casting a critical eye over her curling locks, she tweaked something before nodding with approval. "Perfect."

The Fæ had said nothing when Lamia had stumbled into her suite, hot tears burning her eyes. Nor had she said anything when the girl had flung the knife in the bedside drawer, fumbling to slam it shut.

Instead, she had continued to hang up a dress. A stunning gown of intricate black lace—presumably for that evening's ball. Without a word, she'd ran a bath for her, helping Lamia undress and sink within its warm waters. She had then left her. But, just like a child had an innate ability to sense parental reproach, Lamia had sensed Theodora's disapproval the entire time. A lecture was coming.

Quickly bathing and drying herself, Theodora had then reappeared to help her don the gown, fastening the endless buttons in stony silence. Its halter style hugged her torso and waist before flaring out into a long skirt with a high low hem. On tenterhooks, Lamia had sat patiently as Theodora had tended to her hair. Brushing it with firm strokes to scrap it back into a bushy ponytail.

"Perfect."

Fetching out a shawl of raven feathers, Theodora fastened it about Lamia's shoulders, adjusting it with a critical eye. She then revealed a pair of long black lace gloves and a matching pair of lace knee-high boots.

"What the hell do you think you are doing?" she scolded, suddenly thrusting the gloves into Lamia's hands.

Lamia pulled on the gloves as fiery rage returned to boil her blood. "Did you know he has an Elixium tree?!" she countered heatedly. "Do you know the good it could do?!"

"He uses it for good—" Theodora began before being cut off by the Lamia's angry retort.

"Yeah, I'm sure the 'Forever King' has endless uses for a tree that heals all ailments," she scoffed indignantly.

"Can heal..." Theodora said softly, correcting her.

Lamia stilled, the colour high in her cheeks.

"It doesn't heal all ailments." Without waiting for her to say anything, Theodora reached for her gloved hands, pulling her close. "You lost someone dear to you, didn't you? Did they enter as a Blood Sacrifice?"

Lamia flinched away.

"I've seen how you look at him when he drinks. Why else would you be so hell-bent on revenge? Was he a lover? Your betrothed?" she pressed, her voice earnest yet gentle.

Lamia shook her head, eyes closed in grief. Wrestling with herself, her heart full with a tumult of emotions, she was about to tell her when there was a knock on the door and Hezron appeared. He bowed on seeing them, looking flustered.

"Apologies for disturbing you, Your Majesty, but it is time. The Emperor awaits you at the Throne Room."

Trembling from her inner turmoil, Lamia nodded. "Of course. Thank you, Hezron."

As she turned to follow him, Theodora reached out to take her hand. "Tell him."

Lamia looked horrified.

"Before the court force him to act. And they will. Such behaviour will not be tolerated." Seeing her hesitation, Theodora squeezed her hand reassuringly. "He'll understand. He deserves to know. Now, go."

And, with her words ringing in her ears, Lamia followed Hezron out of her chambers and through the Eternal Palace.

12

Court of The Eternal Palace

She'd half-expected to meet Amias in the Outer Chamber, with its portraits of Myrrithia. But he wasn't there. Slowing as she passed by the many vistas of Myrrithia's wonders, the guards on duty bowed at her approach.

"The Emperor awaits you within, Your Majesty."

And, without another word, they flung open the doors to the Throne Room to reveal the Court of the Eternal Palace. As so many faces turned to look at her, her breath was stolen from her, and she gazed at them in shock, her heart leaping into her throat. It was then she clocked him, standing before his throne at the end of the aisle. He too had changed into an elegant black doublet with matching lace detailing and fitted black trousers that emphasised his physique. He wore his cloak of raven feathers from The Picking, and his dark hair was loose over his shoulders. A simple gold crown adorned his brow. Though his beauty took her breath away, even from where she stood, she could sense an extreme weariness about him. It was almost as if a great age had passed since their last meeting, or a great sadness. His three Felidaeon sat nearby. One nuzzled him in concern.

Guilt tasted bitter in her throat as their eyes met. She glanced down at the floor in shame.

"All hail Queen Lamia! All Hail the Queen of Forever!"

Looking up at the sound of his voice, she saw him raising a hand in her direction. Hezron stood nearby and caught her eye with a look of encouragement. Nodding his head in the direction of the Throne Room, he urged her on as the Emperor's cries were taken up by the court. Walking down the aisle with as much grace and composure as she could muster, she approached the Emperor. It was then she noticed an attendant standing near the Felidaeon holding a cushion. Atop the cushion was a gold crown.

As she neared the dais upon which the Emperor stood, she noticed her parents looking at her with a mixture of awe and pride. Her shame scolded her anew, and she glanced away. Before she could mount the steps of the dais, two guards crossed their halberds, stopping her at its lowest step.

The Emperor and attendant stepped forward.

"Kneel."

At the Emperor's command she knelt, eyeing the halberds warily, Theodora's warning still fresh in her mind.

But, on his command, the guards lifted their halberds, and he took the crown before descending the steps of the dais. Raising the crown up high, Amias addressed the court.

"I crown you Queen of Forever!"

Placing the crown upon her head, the cry 'Queen of Forever' was taken up by the hundreds in attendance. As it echoed through the Throne Room, Amias offered her his hand. Rising to take it with a curtsy, she allowed him to guide her to the throne beside his.

He looked across at her, gaze guarded, as she joined his side.

Heart aching without reason, she stammered a greeting that only he could hear. "My Lord."

"My Queen," he replied, a ghost of a smile softening the lines on his skin until they almost disappeared.

The simple greeting sent a flutter through her chest. Only to have it quashed by grief: she looked away as Theodora's words sprung to mind. She made her eyes meet his. "I'm sorry."

"For what? Almost killing me today or yesterday?"

Abashed, she looked away.

"No matter. I accept your apology. Thank you."

After a moment, she felt his hand squeeze hers. Her gaze flickered up at him in surprise.

"I will tell you," he said, lowering his voice despite the cries ringing out around them. "I will tell you everything you want to know about the Elixium tree, but not tonight. Tomorrow. I promise."

Curious to know why tomorrow was better than that evening, she nodded. "Tomorrow."

"Now," he said, taking a deep breath as if to steady nerves, "let us celebrate your coronation."

"Let us celebrate!" he cried, addressing the courtiers.

Motioning to the footmen standing by a pair of side doors, they were flung open to reveal enchanted candlelight. Music drifted in, a lively and seductive tune that demanded a dance.

She exhaled, easing out the tension from her shoulders, suddenly overcome with a heady mix of nerves and excitement.

As they approached the doors, she felt him bend low, his shoulder grazing hers. The touch was electric.

"I forgot to say how beautiful you are. You have ruined me. You are truly my Queen of Forever."

Stepping out together to the cries of the courtiers, hand in hand, her eyes saw him and only him.

TAKING UP THEIR PLACE in the centre of the dance floor as the court filtered through the double doors, Amias smiled over at Lamia. "The One Who Made the Flowers Bloom is always exceptional. And this time, she is exquisite. The gods have favoured us and I am truly blessed to have Lamia in my life. Though it took several long days... You were all undoubtedly relieved to learn of the success of The Picking. I know my short temper was beginning to vex many of you."

Laughter rippled through the courtiers. Some caught each other's eyes, whilst others hid knowing smiles. Another round of applause began and Amias held Lamia's hand aloft. Her mother and father clapped along with the court, their faces beaming with pride.

Though, despite the merriment, a comment cut through, reaching Lamia's ears and many others. "And continues to until she lets him fuck her."

There was a stony silence as the Emperor held up a sharp hand, his face no longer jovial but dark and icy. His purple gaze glinting with malice. Without a word, he let go of Lamia's hand and stepped towards the crowds. A hush befell the gathered courtiers as he advanced upon a group of women near the back. In the centre was Lady Visha. She looked breathtaking in her silk gown, which hugged her curves. Her blonde hair was piled in an attractive coiffure and displayed the tips of her Fæ ears. She curtsied to the Emperor, sweeping her skirts low to show off her grace and plunging cleavage.

The women about her paled as he stopped before them, hastily copying their friend to curtsy.

"You have something to say, Lady Visha?"

She recovered herself to smile sultrily. "No, My Lord."

"Good." He took an abrupt step forward, catching her throat in his fist. Gasps erupted from those standing close by. "Because, if I catch you spreading any further dirt and spite, I will slit your throat. And, once all the blood has left your body, I shall cast it upon the mountainside for the birds to pick clean. Do you understand?"

She nodded gruffly against his iron grip, gasping for breath. He had almost lifted her clean off her feet.

"And I am your King. Address me as such. Maybe I should send word to your father and ask him to remind you of your manners? You seem to have forgotten yourself. You disgrace yourself and your family."

"Yes, Your Excellency," she panted. "Sorry, Your Excellency!"

Without realising it, Lamia had rushed down the steps after him. Before she knew what she was doing, she'd placed a gentle hand on Amias' arm.

He loosened his hold, and Lady Visha steadied herself with difficulty. When she rose, she glared at Lamia, her eyes blazing.

"Let us dance, My Lord," Lamia said, ignoring her, and she smoothly led him to the middle of the floor.

Catching the hint, Hezron went over to the quartet. The musicians sprang to life and music shattered the silence.

She thought he'd be so incensed that she would have to lead him. But, to her surprise, he placed a tender yet firm hand on the small of her back, his touch sending a wave of warmth through her. Then, gazing down at her, his anger melting to something more intense, he swept her away across the dance floor.

The music and faces and lights blurred as he guided her on several turns of the dance floor, his steps light. His hair fluttered off his shoulders and though she knew she ought to be smiling at the courtiers edging on to the dance floor, she couldn't take her eyes off him.

There was a lull in the music, and Amias brought them to a halt. The court burst into another round of applause. Head spinning, Lamia clapped along with the others before curtsying low in gratitude. Stepping aside, they gestured for others to join them and soon the dance floor was busy with couples dancing to the music.

There was a moment when Amias looked down at Lamia, seeing the colour in her cheeks, and smiled.

Blushing, she was about to thank him for coming to her defence when she caught sight of the three men waiting nearby: Amias' relatives from Elphyne. Sadly, their names eluded her.

Noticing them also, Amias smiled and pulled the older man into a fond embrace. "My Queen, I'm sure you remember King Morozko, my great-nephew on my late elder brother's side. He has been visiting from the Unseelie Court these past two weeks to offer support during The Picking. And this is Prince Aquilo and Prince Boreas, his sons. They depart the day after tomorrow."

The men bowed deeply to her, and Lamia swooped into her most graceful curtsy.

"It's a pleasure to meet you all again," she murmured shyly.

Morozko took her hand in his and kissed the back of it. "The pleasure is ours, Your Majesty. My great-uncle has been graced with much luck this Picking."

She looked up in shock at the coolness of his touch. "Oh!"

Morozko gave a haughty sneer. "Rulers of the Unseelie Court are blessed with Winter's Kiss. It isn't referred to as the Winter Court without reason!"

"Of course," Lamia blushed, averting her gaze from his irises. "You are too kind, Your Majesty. But, 'great-uncle'?"

Amias and Morozko stole a glance at one another.

Boreas, the youngest of the two princes, leaned forward, a conspiratorial glimmer in his snowflake-speckled eyes. He dipped his voice into a mock whisper. "They forget how many 'greats' it really is."

Amias looked bashful.

It was then she spied her parents out of the corner of her eye. With a cry of delight, she leaped into her father's arms, hugging him tight, before grabbing her mother and bringing her into the embrace.

"Oh, darling! How gorgeous you look! We were so excited to hear the news!" Her mother declared, as she drew away to wipe her tears. "Stunned, but excited!"

"And worried!" her father teased.

"Yes, and worried. But we knew you'd be well looked after."

They shyly looked at the Emperor, who stood politely just to the side. As her father bowed, her mother curtsied low, hardly daring to look the Emperor in the face.

"Thank you, Your Excellency, for looking after our daughter. I hope she has been comporting herself well."

The Emperor cast Lamia an indulgent smile. "Impeccably."

Looking away, Lamia had the decency to blush.

Quickly overcoming her shyness, she introduced her parents to the Emperor, who bowed gracefully to them. He then listened indulgently as her mother extolled the finery of the Throne Room, their suite and the celebrations last night.

With Amias entertaining her mother, Lamia stood with her father. He was shaking his head at her in wonder.

"What is it, father?"

"I just cannot believe how gorgeous you look! My daughter... The Queen!"

"Oh, father!" she said, laughing good-naturedly.

"Lamia mentioned that you were here once before, Miklaus?" The Emperor said, gesturing for wine to be brought to them.

"Yes, Your Excellency. You heard a case of ours." Her father bowed, his cheeks warming at the Emperor using his name.

"I hope the matter was resolved?" Amias enquired, as he handed them each a glass of wine. Though he took none for himself.

"Yes, Your Excellency. It was closed most satisfactorily. In fact, it brought us much trade."

"Oh, I am pleased."

As the men began talking business and politics, Delilah linked arms with her daughter, leading her in a turn of the ballroom. The dance floor was full and the atmosphere of the room was bright and cheerful. People either stood and chattered amiably with one another or could be found playing cards.

"Well, my dear, what a turn of events! I never could have imagined it!"

"Thanks!"

Her mother laughed, squeezing her arm. "You know what I mean. What was it like?"

And Lamia described her journey through the palace, the Chapel and The Picking. Conveniently missing out her multiple attempts at killing the Emperor.

Her mother's eyes widened. "Oh, my! What an adventure! And the flowers returned to life once more?" she asked, lifting her daughter's hand to see the cut across its palm. Clasping it, she brought it to her lips and kissed it, with tears glistening in her eyes. "I always knew you were special. Both you and your brother."

"You have a brother?"

Lamia jumped at the sound of Amias' voice just to her side. Flustered, the two ladies bobbed hastily.

"Had, Your Excellency," Miklaus said as a sadness befell his wife. "Lamia had a twin brother, but he... he died... Last year..."

Amias cast her a questioning look, but she avoided his piercing gaze.

Delilah cleared her throat, forcing a smile. "He, erh, was a Blood Sacrifice actually, Your Excellency. You accepted his application last year. He... he left us soon after the summer solstice."

A Blood Sacrifice...

He looked at her, eyes widening with realisation.

Avoiding his gaze, Lamia wiped her eyes with the back of her hand. Miklaus and Delilah glanced at one another, trying to smile, though their mutual grief weighed down heavy on them.

Miklaus reached for his wife's hand and gave it a reassuring squeeze. "His name was Lathan, Your Excellency. He was dying of cancer and was in much pain prior to being accepted as a Blood Sacrifice."

Lamia didn't know where to look. The grief that always preyed on her was barely tolerable. The joy she'd felt whilst dancing in Amias' arms was a distant memory as she thought back to her brother. She blinked away the tears, the pain in her chest almost crippling.

She started in surprise to find a cool hand seeking hers, fingers threading through to intertwine with hers. Bringing her hand up, Amias kissed it gently.

Their eyes met and though she expected scorn, she found compassion.

"I see. Please accept my deepest sympathy for your loss. I know it is hard felt."

It was too much.

Closing her eyes, she felt the tears overspill to course down her cheeks.

A touch appeared on her cheek, light and reverent as it wiped away the tear. "I understand..."

Before anyone could say anything more, there was a soft cough. Looking, they found a butler carrying a gold tray, upon which was a note sealed with blue wax with two hands holding a tree embossed there: the insignia of the Healers. The butler bowed deeply as they offered the tray to the Emperor.

At first, Amias did nothing. Then, letting go of Lamia's hand, he reached for the paper, opening it reluctantly, as if he weren't sure whether he wanted to see its contents.

As he read whatever was there, lines of grief reappeared, making Lamia's heart twist with something she couldn't explain.

He replaced the note. "Please excuse me. I am afraid I must see to matters of court, My Queen." He bowed to Lamia's parents. "Mother, Father, please make yourselves comfortable. You are welcome to stay as long as you wish. You are family now."

Lamia's parents bowed in response, looking slightly flustered.

He turned to go, stopping when Lamia reached for him. She felt him shudder at her touch. "Where are you going, My Lord?"

Silently, he led her through a set of side doors into a corridor with windows along its exterior walls. Moonlight spilled in through their glass, scattering shadows about. The doors shut behind them and he almost stumbled.

"Amias!" Lamia cried, steadying him. "What's wrong?"

She somehow hadn't thought to see the vampire emperor in such a state. It frightened her. Surely someone so old and without concern for mortal ways could never be so moved by anything?

With a swiftness that took her breath away, he grabbed her, hand sliding round her neck, lifting her face up to meet his. Meeting his eyes, she was stunned to see tears there.

"Amias?"

His eyes lightened at the sound of his name upon her lips and he smiled a soft, sad smile. "I see you, Lamia Fontaine. I see you."

And without another word, he kissed her. Gently at first, lips so tender against hers it made her heart ache, then feeling her pulse quicken under his thumb, he kissed her more deeply as if she were a lifeline, an anchor keeping him grounded through a storm. As if he feared she might disappear at any moment. She gasped as his lips crashed against hers with increasing ferocity, feeling him gently squeeze her throat, finger and thumb trickling along it. She quivered, ripples shuddering through her all the way to her core. The wild memory of his fangs brushing her skin came to mind, and she was suddenly desperate to feel them against her now, heat igniting within her groin. Forgetting everything, she pulled him closer, gripping onto him, only to find him pulling reluctantly away, lips red.

His gaze collided with hers, hot with longing. "I must go," he said, voice breaking as he made to depart.

"Take me with you!" she blurted, worry overwhelming her.

He hesitated, glancing from her to the end of the corridor. "I will, I promise. But not today. Be with your family. Be happy. Time with loved ones is so precious."

And he swept off down the corridor.

13

Blood Sacrifice

Re-entering the hall, Lamia found people dancing. Laughter and gaiety cut through the air, a stark contrast to the worries of the Emperor and the dark corridor he'd disappeared down.

"Darling? Is everything well?" her father asked.

They were waiting for her near the door, watching the spectacle of the gathering.

"I-I'm not sure," she replied, worrying her lip. Her mind was a-whirl.

"I'm sure the Emperor has everything in hand," her mother said confidently.

Without Amias, Lamia felt suddenly overwhelmed by the hustle and bustle of the court. She felt her mother's arm link with hers.

"Let us excuse ourselves. I should love to show you the suite His Excellency has prepared for us. I would have shown you this morning, but we were a little worse for wear following last night's celebrations."

"*I* was quite well," her father said, a twinkle in his eye. "It was your mother who fared badly. You know what she is like with champagne."

Lamia nodded, blinking away tears. "Yes, I should like that."

Before she'd even taken a step, Theodora and Hezron appeared at her side.

The Fæ girl smiled. "Are you retiring, Your Majesty?"

"Yes, I am going to visit my parents' suite." She turned to her mother. "Mother, this is Theodora, my Maid-in-Waiting," Lamia said, introducing her.

"Oh! You're the one who worked wonders with her hair!" Delilah exclaimed.

A smug smile broke out over Theodora's lips. "Well, when you put it like that."

"Come," said Hezron, "let us give your parents a tour, Your Majesty."

CONDUCTING A TOUR OF the palace as they made their way to the Queen's Suite where her parents were staying, Hezron revealed himself to be a fountain of knowledge. He knew much of the palace and its curios, and told some fascinating tales of their origins and how they ended up in the Emperor's collections. Finally, he and Theodora brought them to a splendid suite in white with gold gilt. It was almost identical to the one Lamia shared with Amias, but smaller and without the circular window overlooking the city of Dårath. A bouquet of roses was arranged on a table amongst a cluster of settees and chairs that stood before a fire. Their sweet scent filled the room.

Her father then left them to smoke his pipe in the gardens. With Hezron standing guard outside, Theodora helped Lamia remove the headpiece as Delilah settled herself onto a settee. The door opened, and a maid bearing a tray with a pot of flower tea entered.

"I took the liberty of requesting a pot of camomile tea and some light refreshment for you, Your Majesty. There is some homemade honey, too."

"Thank you," Lamia said with a smile of appreciation as she settled next to her mother.

Pouring them each a cupful, Theodora and the maid then left them alone.

Delilah caught Lamia's eyes. Lamia smiled to see the excitement and awe. Giggling like schoolgirls, Delilah scooped a hearty spoonful of honey into each of their cups and poured out the tea.

"Well, I have to say I never envisaged this!" Delilah declared after a moment of savouring the soothing sweetness of the tea.

Lamia offered her mother a homemade biscuit. "Life has certainly taken a surprising turn."

"That's an understatement!" Delilah scoffed before eyeing her carefully. "My daughter, the Queen of Noxterra! And, are you... happy?"

Lamia gazed into the golden depths of the tea in her hands. *She hadn't been happy in months.*

Delilah took another biscuit. "The Emperor seems quite pleasant. Very polite! And so much more attractive than the rumours say!"

Lamia blushed. "He's been most kind."

Delilah nodded encouragingly, expecting more. "And, erm, your wedding night was agreeable?"

Turning away, Lamia's blush deepened.

She raised an eyebrow. "That good!"

Squirming in her seat, Lamia played with her lace skirts, adjusting them unnecessarily.

Paling, her mother looked at her sorrowfully. "It wasn't, erh, agreeable?"

"No, no, nothing like that. It, erh, didn't happen..."

"Oh, but my dear! Why?" She placed a hand on Lamia's arm.

Lamia felt the heat rise in her cheeks.

"Do, erh, his preferences lie elsewhere?" she asked in hushed tones.

Lamia reddened even more. "No, nothing like that!"

"Well, nerves are very common. For men and women," she said reassuringly. "The Emperor appears a patient man. Has he, erm... been gentle in his advances?"

Lamia nodded stiffly.

"I can imagine he knows his way around—"

"Mother!"

"I was just saying," she said, feigning innocence, though her smile told a different story.

Lamia couldn't believe she was having this conversation with her own mother!

"You're as incorrigible as Theodora," Lamia sighed with a weary laugh.

"I like Theodora."

"I do, too," Lamia agreed.

"So, why haven't you? Is it because you prefer women?"

Lamia shook her head, meeting her mother's eyes reluctantly. "I couldn't bring myself to..."

"She's been far too preoccupied with trying to kill him than to ride him."

They looked up in astonishment at Theodora's candid tones. She was leading an entourage of servants bearing numerous gowns. After directing them to place them within the wardrobes, she joined the two ladies on the settee and sat down with a sigh.

Delilah leaned forward. "She's not being serious? You're not being serious?" she asked, rounding on Lamia before Theodora could reply.

Lamia hid behind her hands.

"No!" Delilah covered her mouth with her hand, her eyes round.

Theodora nodded and poured herself a cup of camomile tea. "Four times, from what I know."

"'Four times'?!" Delilah's eyes widened ever more—if that was possible.

Lamia remained hidden behind her hands.

"He'll have you killed! You can't go around trying to assassinate him! Why?"

Lamia removed her hands to reveal tears trickling down her cheeks.

"He killed Lathan, mother! How can I give myself to him?!"

Her mother paled.

Theodora looked over the rim of her teacup, a shrewd gaze flickering from Lamia to her mother. "Might I ask who Lathan was?"

Delilah regained her composure with difficulty and gave a tight smile that failed to meet her eyes. When she tried to speak, no words would come. Clearing her throat, she tried again. "Lathan was my son and Lamia's twin. H-he died as a Blood Sacrifice."

With all the pieces falling into place, Theodora looked at Lamia with a sad smile.

Mustering her courage, Delilah blinked away tears and took her daughter's hand in hers. "No, my darling, he didn't. He tried to save him."

Lamia looked at her in confusion.

"He didn't! Lathan came here and the Emperor, he..." Lamia trailed off, unable to finish for the horrors of what a Blood Sacrifice must go through. *Did they strap them down when they drained their blood? Or did they suck the blood straight out of them? And did it hurt?*

Theodora had been watching her with keen hazel eyes. "Do you know what it involves? Being a Blood Sacrifice?"

Lamia shook her head. "Not really. Only the rumours I've heard."

"Which are probably exaggerated lies at the best of times," Theodora snorted in disdain.

Delilah caught the Fæ girl's eyes.

Theodora nodded. "I shall arrange for you to see the Blood Sacrifices."

"What? No! I don't want to see them!"

"You must, Your Majesty. Only then will you understand," she smiled reassuringly. "In any case, the Hospital Wing is a pleasant place, and I know the Wards are interested in meeting their new queen just as much as everyone else."

"Mother?" Lamia asked cautiously, turning to her mother.

Delilah was sitting with her head bowed, hand clenched against her chest. When she looked up, her eyes, though still filled with tears, were bright. "I think that's a marvellous idea. Lathan would be so proud. And," she said, a glimmer of mischief appearing as she caught Theodora's eye, "we must also do something to smite Lady Visha's cruel rumours!"

"Leave it to me, ma'am," Theodora said.

AN HOUR LATER, SHE found herself in her own suite, after having bid her parents goodnight.

Theodora and Hezron had accompanied her back through the palace. The light of the twin moons had cut through the windows, scattering pearlescent reflections across the walls and floor.

Once they were safely within her suite, Theodora had helped her bathe and change, chatting amiably about her parents, the gathering and Lady Visha.

"She'll be lucky to see another season here. The Emperor has little time for scheming."

"Surely he's used to it?" Lamia asked in surprise, waiting as Theodora brushed her hair.

"Just because he's immortal doesn't mean he enjoys senseless spite. Lady Visha is a vindictive cow. He's only put up with her thus far because she is Fæ and daughter to Baron Dunbarrow, who has links to his home in Elphyne."

"I don't think she likes me..."

"Of course not. Before your arrival, she had designs on the Emperor. Everyone knew."

"'Designs' on him?! Do you, do you mean they were lovers?"

For some reason, the thought sent a cold fury burning through Lamia's veins.

"I doubt it, Your Majesty. Is anything the matter?" Theodora regarded her carefully.

Lamia forced a smile. "No, everything's fine."

"There!" Theodora exclaimed, standing back to admire her handiwork.

"I look like a woman from the red quarters!" Lamia declared, turning on her heel to look at her reflection for the first time. Theodora had put her in a sheer halter neck gown with a backless low-cut bodice and artfully placed lace trimmings and decorations. She'd never felt so exposed, despite its trailing skirts.

Or sexy.

"Good!" Theodora said, lightning candles before extinguishing the torches with a flick of her wrist.

"What?!"

"Let me know how you get on." She gave a coy wink before gathering up her things and heading for the door.

Lamia watched her leave in astonishment.

Casting her reflection one last look—a thrill ran through her as she imagined how the Emperor would react—she went over to the bed.

She sat down tentatively. It was a lot softer than her bed at home. Deciding to wait up for him, she opened the bedside drawer and fetched out the knife she'd taken from him at the Elixium tree. It was an exquisite piece, well balanced, with deceptively sharp edges. Its handle was metal with decorated reliefs of leaves and branches twisting along it.

Deciding to return it to him, she placed it on the tabletop and waited, her insides squirming with nerves. It was then she caught sight of the slash across her palm. Theodora had been most attentive, cleaning and applying ointment, so it no longer stung, though it still looked red. She thought of the mad whirlwind of the last two days. Two days where her life had permanently and unequivocally changed.

She glanced over at the roses in their vase, her insides twisted with guilt at their dishevelled appearance. They held none of their splendour as when she'd first revived them during The Picking.

It was like some fairy tale, she thought, shaking her head. What was it he had said?

It is the life-force in my Queen's blood that I need to sire children...

Something in *her* blood.

Maybe it could work again?

Taking the blade, she approached the vase of flowers. Jabbing its point against the cut on her palm, she bit her lip as the skin broke and crimson blossomed. Quickly holding the hand over the vase, she watched as the blood dribbled down and round the curve of her palm before *drip dripping* into the water. She watched the drops diffuse as bloody wisps.

The blood looked normal enough.

She waited expectedly, not daring to breathe, but nothing happened. No glow or shimmer of magic came.

She sighed.

Returning the knife to the bedside table once more, she washed the blood off her hand, dabbing it clean before turning to look at the bed.

He wouldn't be long...

Could tonight be the night?

Her mother had insisted she stopped trying to kill the Emperor and tried seducing him instead. Admittedly, it was a challenge she was rather looking forward to. She thought of his broad shoulders, taut muscles, long hair, and soft lips. A thrill ran through her as she imagined his touch once more upon her skin...

I mean, couldn't she have him if she wanted him? He was her husband, as much as she was his wife. If she wanted him, she could have him.

Stretching out upon the bed, she rested her head on her hand, allowing her other to droop seductively—she hoped—over her hip.

Not that her mother had elaborated how she should go about seducing him, but surely this would be a good start?

Though Lamia knew little about the relations between a husband and wife, she was getting an idea of what was involved. And, she admitted, she wanted more. With the Emperor, even. Despite what had happened to Lathan. Despite what he was.

I see you, Lamia Fontaine. I see you...

She shuddered at the echo of his declaration. Its magnitude moving her core in ways she had never realised or knew she wanted.

He saw her.

He knew her.

And, dare she say it, she wanted to see him, too.

AFTER WAITING FOR WHAT felt an age, the cold settling uncomfortably on her, the Emperor had still not appeared. Resisting the urge to pull the covers over and give in to sleep, she decided to return to the Library and fetch some reading material.

Opening the door to find Hezron on guard, she explained her need for a book. Politely averting his gaze from her revealing attire, he allowed her to lead the way. Enchanted torches burned from their sconces on the walls, casting shimmering shadows through their depths. Thinking back to her earlier tours, she made her way to the Central Court, slipping through the palace quietly, not wanting to draw attention to herself.

It wasn't late, but there was little sound of revelry—the court must have retired for the evening. Catching a glimpse of Myrrithia's twin moons through the windows, Lamia could see they were at their highest point: midnight.

Arriving at the Central Court, she exited via the side door Amias had taken her through earlier that day. Before her lay the corridor leading to the Library. With a victorious smile, she opened its door. She stopped short in surprise at seeing a fire lit in its grate. Torches burned brightly from their sconces.

"Amias?" she called hopefully, leaving Hezron outside.

Hearing no answer, she walked over to the desk to find a file open upon it. Sheets of parchment lay scattered about the surface. And, staring back at her, was a sketch of her brother.

She stopped short, head whirling, and stumbled round for a better look. Whoever had sketched him had caught the softness of his eyes, and the stubborn tilt to his chin. She felt a sob tickle her throat and quickly wiped away her tears.

Reaching, she scanned the documents. They included what looked like applications. One was in her brother's hand—achingly familiar. Lamia ran a loving hand over its flowing calligraphy. It detailed why he wished to be considered for a Blood Sacrifice. The second one included a detailed evaluation of his illness. Annotations in an elegant hand, filled the margins. There was a form below it entitled: 'Medical Treatment' with a list of dates and medication tried—tinctures from the Elixium tree. One word had been noted by all attempts: 'FAILURE'.

Her brother had received treatment prior to being a Blood Sacrifice?

She frowned. She remembered regular deliveries for her brother in the months prior to his announcement that he was going to be a Blood Sacrifice. But she had assumed they were from their local Healer in Gerran, not the palace itself. And certainly not from the Elixium tree.

Was this the same for all Blood Sacrifices? Did the Healers try to cure them before their applications were approved?

Sure enough, underneath the record of treatment, a stamp with 'APPLICATION APPROVED' had been inked across a final form with Lathan's signature, giving his consent to become a Blood Sacrifice upon his death. A number had then been written: 86789.

But why hadn't tinctures from the tree worked?

Spying more notes on her brother's treatment whilst at the palace, she was about to read on when she heard the hushed chatter of servants.

Scurrying to the door, she spied the retreating forms of two servants making their way down the corridor. They were carrying basins of water and one full of bloodied cloths between them.

"The poor dear," one said, sniffling.

"I know, to have borne so much at such a tender age." The other dabbed their eyes with their free hand.

"Hopefully, she is at peace now."

"It's good that her parents could be there."

"His Excellency insists on it for all minors, unless the parents are estranged."

"He's a wreck."

"The death of all Blood Sacrifices hits him hard, especially that of children."

Lamia watched them exit via a door and looked the way they had come. Mind made up, she indicated for Hezron to wait before tiptoeing down the corridor, keeping close to the wall. After a couple of minutes, she found herself in a long corridor. At the far end was a door that was familiar...

The Chapel!

And close by was an arched doorway with a relief of two hands holding a tree upon its keystone: the mark of the Healers.

The door was slightly ajar.

Unable to resist, Lamia crept across, sidling along it to peek through the gap.

There upon an altar, surrounded by hundreds of candles, lay the body of a young girl, her long dark hair flowing over the headrest like ink. Even from her vantage point, Lamia could tell she was no longer breathing. Besides her horrifically sallow skin, there was the distinct feeling of emptiness to her. That, whatever vivacious life force the girl had once possessed, was now no more.

And there, leaning over her by the flickering light of the candles, was the Emperor.

Horror-stricken, Lamia fell through the door. "Amias! What are you doing?!"

Amias jerked his head up, his purple eyes wide with shock at seeing her there.

She froze, taking in his puffy eyes and the tears glittering within them.

He'd been crying?!

"Lamia! What are you doing here?" His eyes skimmed her revealing gown in a mixture of surprise and awe. "And why are you dressed like that outside of our bedchamber?"

Lowering the candelabra just a little, she ignored the colour warming her cheeks and stuck out her chin, determined to win back some semblance of control. "I came looking for you, of course. What are you doing over the body of a dead girl?"

The Emperor reached for the child, tucking a lock of hair behind her ear.

"Her name is Felicity... Was Felicity... Ward 87158. She was only six... She died but an hour ago. Her parents have just left, but I... I wanted to sit with her... Just a while longer... Before..."

Six... The poor thing...

"We try to cure them... We use the Elixium tree to try to cure them. Sometimes it works, but sometimes... Sometimes it doesn't..."

He turned away from the girl, his face crumpling with grief, eyes squinting shut.

Lamia stared at him in amazement. This vampire, this God of Death, this King of Forever, *mourned* them! "Y-you sit with them?"

He nodded, hand covering his eyes. "I visit the Hospital Wing daily, but when a Ward passes, I like to be with them until the end."

She felt like an arrow had pierced her chest. Clutching the pain, biting back the tears, she lowered the candelabra. "Were you... Were you there with my brother? When he died?"

Amias met her eyes, the pain clear to see. "Yes, I was there."

The candelabra slipped from her hands as her knees gave way. Then the next thing she knew, she was on all fours. The cold flagstones beneath her as her grief broke, and she wailed, sobs ripping through her at the memory of her brother. Her darling, wonderful, brilliant brother...

Arms appeared around her, enveloping her with unexpected strength and warmth as she cried uncontrollably. Without a word, he held her tight, his grief mingling with hers as the candlelight swathed them in their warmth.

14

I See You

After leaving the girl with the Healers for blood letting, Amias took Lamia on a tour of the Hospital Wing while covering her shoulders with his jacket. The Wards were excited to see their new queen, passing on their congratulations as Lamia walked along row after row of comfortable beds. Skylights had been cut into the ceiling, allowing the Wards to see the heavens as they changed day in, day out. At present, stars twinkled down at them, and the twin moons of Myrrithia hung bright in the dark skies.

Exiting the Hospital Wing, they entered a corridor with several more dormitories veering off from it. Taking her hand, he led her through a grander set of doors gilded with gold, and Lamia found herself in a forest.

Taken aback, she froze, craning her neck as she followed the trees up to their crowns high above. Stars glistened through their leaves. Frowning, it was then she noticed the iron arches and glass and realised they were in a giant glass house.

She stepped out onto a lawn scattered with wildflowers, marvelling at the soft grass underfoot. "This is..." she began, but words failed her.

He smiled to see her astonishment, and taking her hand in his, led her into the forest. She could smell the damp grass and soil and the heady scent of flowers. It was then she spied white stones of a similar

131

height laid out in rows amidst the grass. Each one bore a name and a number: gravestones. And, as they passed them, he spoke of them...

"Dragomir liked painting. He painted the most wonderful landscapes. And Tammany had the most exquisite of singing voices. She would often sing for us in the evening..."

Heart in her throat, she stumbled after him as he remembered the different Wards, recalling their quirks and talents. Then, slowing to a halt, he stopped in front of a gravestone bearing the name 'Lathan Fontaine', and the number 86789.

Her brother...

Suddenly, the pain was overwhelming. She collapsed to her knees and bowed down before the stone, sobbing.

"Whilst we return much of their ash to their families for burial, a handful is retained for our own funeral service."

"You held a funeral for him, too?" she stammered, staring at the white stone with her brother's name upon it.

"Of course." He knelt next to her and placed a hand on the small of her back, soothing in its strength. "He passed away quickly, with dignity and no pain. I was there like I am for all Wards who pass on. He was so brave."

She nodded, unable to respond.

"I should've noticed it, the family resemblance. You remind me of him: brave and fierce."

Her tear-soaked eyes sought him then.

"I-I do?"

He nodded, smoothing away a lock of hair from her cheeks. "Only his sister would attempt to kill me thrice."

"Four times," she said, shying away; the heat rising in her cheeks.

"Who's counting?" he chuckled, eyes bright. "And I adore you for it. I knew you were special the moment you appeared in the Chapel. They don't suffer," he continued. "The Elixium tree is used to try to heal them. Sometimes it works, and the Healers manage to save the patient, but sometimes it doesn't... It's then used to create tonics for pain relief. To give them dignity in death."

"I saw the file."

"You did?"

"I went looking for a book to read," she explained. "I remember the packages arriving home. I just assumed they were from the local Healer, not from here."

"Once I approve an application, they come under my care."

"But, why? Why do it?"

He looked thoughtful. "A long, long time ago, when I liberated Noxterra, I discovered the Elixium tree. In all my travels, I had never seen one. It was in a poor way. People had pilfered from it, ransacking it until it was close to dying, killing others to keep it for themselves... It was then I knew I had to stay, to protect it. I have no need for it, so I am the best sort of custodian. So, I settled here, and ruled Noxterra, claiming the tree for my own to preserve and keep it safe.

"With time and nurture, it grew strong and healed and, over the centuries, it fell out of memory... I knew I had to use it for good, but in a controlled way that kept it safe whilst helping others. So, I built the temple to protect it and opened up spaces for Blood Sacrifices. A way to help those with the greatest need, whilst also allowing my kind to exist without needless killing. Being immortal, I felt it was my duty to guard it. The tree has helped countless thousands. Some illnesses cannot be cured, but many can and their survivors live on to enjoy long and happy lives. That makes it worthwhile."

"That's why you stayed in Noxterra?"

He gave her a half-smile that sent her insides fluttering. "It was hardly for the scenery. I grew up in the forests of Elphyne, amidst greenery and trees, not mountainous outcrops. Though its lack of sunlight is beneficial for my life."

There was a pause as Lamia gazed at her brother's tombstone, mind reeling from Amias' revelations.

"Thank you," she found herself saying.

It was his time to shy away. "You're most welcome. I just wish the Elixium tree had been able to heal him. For your family's sake."

"But thank you for trying."

"And... I wish there was more I could do. For your sake..."

She looked at him in surprise. A soft smile was on his lips and, this time, he didn't shy away from her gaze.

"You have done so much already," she said, the words spilling from her. "I was so angry. At him for succumbing to the illness. At the world for giving it to him. And at you for taking him away... But I'm not angry anymore... It's like a weight has been lifted and I can finally breathe."

"For that, I am glad. I find myself caring for you. A great deal. There is little I would refuse if it guaranteed your happiness."

Biting back more tears, she leaned against his chest. He looked pleasantly surprised and tentatively settled her into the crook of his neck.

They sat like that, for the longest of moments, in front of her brother's stone, the stars blazing high overhead through the branches of the trees.

The enormity of his care for the Wards humbled her. She now understood why he kept the Elixium tree safe. He was right, unprotected, it would be ransacked by humans. Guarded like it was, he could use it to try to heal those with life-threatening illnesses.

She understood.

Pulling away, she looked at him, hand reaching for his cheek. "Amias de Marc, I see you."

He shuddered against her touch. "You see me?" His voice wobbled, a torrent of emotions laid bare upon his fine features. He looked like he might say something, but not trusting himself, swallowed back the lump in his throat.

"I see you," she repeated, smiling.

He inhaled sharply before drawing her into a strong embrace, crushing her against him as she clung to him. Before she knew what she was doing, she'd wrapped her fingers around the nape of his neck and drew him down until their lips were but a whisper away. Then, eyes closing, she brushed them with hers. They were as soft as she remembered them. Sighing against her, he kissed her back, gently at first, before tentatively teasing her with his tongue.

She opened her mouth and let him in.

Panting at the sudden intimacy, they kissed with increased desperation. Their mouths crashed against one another, their tongues hungrily exploring the other. An urgency had awoken within her: she was hungry. Hungry for the taste of him. Hungry for the feel of him as her hands roamed his chest and shoulders, coasting over the wings of his shoulder blades as they travelled down his spine.

He untied his tunic, exposing the bare toned muscles of his chest as he tossed the garment behind her. She paused, looking down at him, taking in his grooves and curves as her fingers traced their lines. Firm and warmer than she'd expected. Biting her lip, her gaze met his, his purple eyes glowing with a smouldering intensity that sent her senses spiralling into an inferno. Threading her fingers through his silky hair, pulling him close, she kissed him deeply once more. Sighing against his caress that left goosebumps in its wake. Her body overflowing with needs she hadn't realised existed. She needed him closer, needed to feel him naked against her.

Working on instinct, she shrugged off his jacket with his help, letting him sit her in his lap. Wrapping her legs around his waist, she felt the throb of his manhood straining against his breeches. So close... So tantalisingly close... Her whole being thrummed with an uncontrollable energy, culminating in her groin where it built up with a crazed thirst.

I see you...

His hands stroked her, setting her aflame as their touch trailed along her back and the curve of her bum and thigh. Squeezing her, making her feel every inch desirable as they caressed her flesh. Feeling his hands appear on the swell of her hips sent a current jolting through her and she gasped, squirming against his crotch. Biting back a moan, he fumbled with her gown, pulling the collar down to reveal her breasts. Kissing her, she felt him cup their luscious curves in the palms of his hands. He brushed them, taking their nipples between a finger and thumb to roll and knead and whip her into a frenzy. Leaning, his mouth found their peaks, licking and sucking them with lips and tongue, tracing their bumps and grooves with languid wantonness. Letting his fangs graze them...

She threw back her head, a cry escaping her lips as a current tingled through her. The delight was exquisite!

With her neck exposed, he drew her close, licking and sucking its gentle curve, letting his fangs skim along its surface with measured care. Enough to tease. Enough to enthral. Focusing on the skin where her jaw neared her ear, she groaned to feel his panting breath caressing her, loud and hungry.

"Do you want me to stop?" his voice rumbled, guttural and hoarse within his throat. "Tell me to stop and I will."

She shook her head, unable to fathom why she should want him to stop such a pleasurable thing.

"You want me?" he said, lips kissing her jawline. She moaned. "Do you want me, Lamia? Do you want me to make you a goddess amongst women?"

He was all around her, his touch, his breath, the feel of his bare muscles, the throb of his cock. He was everywhere and in everything. She could taste him on her tongue. She could smell him and his desire.

"Because, once I'm in, you're mine."

"I want you, Amias. I want you." She heard herself whisper, head too dizzy with pleasure, too overwhelmed with anticipation to resist him, this man, this god of death who cared for her.

Straddling him harder. Pressing him closer, he hissed at the feel of her. Kissing her, she took his face in her hands as he pushed her down, lowering her against the cushion of grass and clothing. Bunching up the lacey skirts of her gown, he moved them out of the way, burying his head against the heat of her undergarments. Squealing with delight, she laughed as he took them in his teeth, ripping them away.

"Let's see how wet you are..."

She gasped as he gently slipped a finger within her, the sensation new and beautiful. Stroking her clitoris, he fondled it in gentle circles.

"Oh, yes!" he exclaimed. "My, aren't you wet, wife?"

She stilled, eyes rolling back into her head as pleasurable waves rippled through her. Then, before she knew what he was doing, he'd buried his face within her softness.

"Oh, my!" she breathed, clutching the grass against the pleasure.

She could feel his lips worshipping her, and his tongue exalting her as it slipped further inside, hot and wet and warm. Unhurriedly exploring her, holding her ass in place with his hands, he fed, sucking on her, licking her inside and out as she groaned and squirmed and wheezed his name, hands clawing along his back as they tried for a purchase amidst the whirlwind of desire that had her within its clutches. Even if she wanted to, which she most *definitely* didn't, she wouldn't have been able to resist him. Not now. Probably not ever.

She was his.

Even if theirs wasn't to be a love match. Even if he was wicked, she wanted every last inch of him.

In her.

Above her.

Under her.

Emerging, eyes drunk with her taste, he wiped his mouth with the back of his hand and crawled forward, covering her body with his. As he braced himself on either side of her, his eyes roamed her, hooded with desire. He let his lips brush hers with tangible need. She could taste herself on them.

"I want you to remember every detail of me inside you..." His black hair fell from his shoulders, enshrouding them. "Are you ready for me, my wife? My Queen? My Everything?"

He was all she could see. The soft glow of his eyes, bright like a predator. The gentle curve of his lip.

My Everything?

She nodded, feeling delirious as anxiety and desire shivered through her in equal measure.

And he kissed her fervently as he fumbled with the ties to his breeches. Knowing his hardness lay just out of reach, she helped him, yanking his garment down and away. Feeling the curve of his bum, stroking it in smooth circles. He had such an amazing ass. She gripped it hard, and he laughed, impatiently kicking aside his breeches.

"You like my ass?"

"It's grown on me..." she admitted coyly.

"Good."

Looking down, unable to resist seeing him in all his glory, she groaned to see the size of him. If she thought he'd been huge the other day, that was nothing to what he was now.

"That's all for you, Lamia. That is what you do to me."

She gazed at his cock. "I don't think it's going to fit."

He laughed, a low throaty laugh. "I have ways of making it fit."

He eyed her, lain down against the grass and clothes, her hair splayed out across the greenery and flowers like some black halo. Her cheeks were rosy with desire, and her eyes dilated with passion. She ought to feel shy. Instead, she felt desired and immensely sexy. An unknown wantonness came over her and she found her hands gliding over her own curves. Cupping her breasts and squeezing them as he watched on, his eyes keenly tracing their journey across her collarbone and breasts, the tender swell of her stomach and the softness of her thighs. As she approached her womanhood, he smiled a soft, sultry smile and leant forward. "By the gods, I am blessed. I promise to worship you. With every breath... With all that I am..."

Her eyes involuntarily flickered to his dick, jutting forward, almost touching her.

"Do you want me?"

She nodded, mesmerised. "I want you."

"Now?"

"Most definitely now."

Taking her hands in his, entwining their fingers, he braced himself over her, pinning her hands by her head. He let his cock tease her, its tip slowly entering her. His eyes never left hers, desperate to catch every second.

Feeling herself stretch open for him, welcome his hardness inch by tantalising impossible inch, she watched him, groaning against the sensation of her, whilst her own breath hitched at the feel of his throbbing cock sliding into her, stealing away all sense, her very ability to think.

And he kept going.

By the gods, he kept going!

She let out a mew of excitement at the feel of him slipping deeper inside her with such delicious ease. "Amias!"

"Take me. All of me," he pleaded, eyes burning, jaws clenched against the passion building up within him. The bliss that lay just out of reach.

Easing her legs apart with his, he released her hands to raise her hips so that they rested upon his thighs and pulled her close. She inhaled sharply to feel him slide further in. Embedding himself within her.

"To the hilt," he breathed. "Take me to the hilt." Shuddering as he slid home. Her eyes rolled back into her head. "By the gods, you're tight!"

Gasping, she looked at him, their eyes meeting in breathless wonder and Lamia had the sudden feeling of being complete. Had they been made for one another, fitting together so? He smiled a soft secret smile, and she felt her heart fill to bursting.

Could this be more than mere sex?

The softness of his look melted away, though, as a predatory feline air took over. A wicked smile curled his lips, his fangs flashing. He was poised to attack. And there was nothing she could do. She was entirely at his mercy.

The thrill was glorious.

"I promised I'd make you scream my name," he purred, moving out slowly, only to slide back in. "And I keep my promises."

She shuddered at the delight of it, his dick throbbing inside her like some wild animal barely contained.

Hands on her hips, he physically guided her off his shaft, almost to its tip, then, before he left her, just as slowly, he pulled her back towards him, along his length until her ass sat snug against his crotch.

She groaned, eyes fluttering shut.

"Good?"

She nodded, biting her lip coyly as she reopened her eyes. The pupils were dilated and a dreamy look was on her face.

"Good."

And he did it again, slowly, so excruciatingly slow that she felt every pit and grove and pulse of his cock pulling and pushing in and out of her.

And he did it again.

And again.

And again.

With each slow, calculated thrust, a wave of heat ricocheted through her groin, up her spine, and back again.

He withdrew, not all the way, just far enough to watch his dick appear soaked with her juices, before allowing it to disappear once more within her mound.

As he entered her again, he shut his eyes, breathing slowly, bracing himself against whatever sensation he felt—was it as sublime as the waves rushing through her?

She hoped so. She sincerely hoped so.

He sighed, a shuddering sigh that left her breathless.

"Perfect...," she heard him say. "Never before has it... felt so... perfect!"

With that final exclamation, he swiftly drew her to him, gathering her in his lap so they faced each other. The sudden change of position brought him against a particularly sensitive spot, taking her breath away.

Mind whirling, she felt him thrust up and up, harder and deeper, faster and stronger. Like an animal unleashed.

He was so deep! So hard!

Locking her legs around him, she held on tight, gripping his shoulders and neck, throwing her head back as he fucked her. Pulling away, he bent to her neck, licking it and sucking it in time with each thrust. Grazing along his fangs along her neck, she moaned and panted his name over and over. Something was happening. These delicious ripples were growing and growing. She could feel them taking over. Part of her was nervous, but part of her sensed something magnificent was about to happen and she wanted it to come sooner. She craved it.

He must have sensed it too, for he kissed her. Covering her gasps with his mouth as the tension built, letting his fangs trail over her neck and bosom, the swell of her breasts... She groaned against the delight.

"Oh! Oh, Amias!"

"Scream my name," he panted. "It's all yours."

Her hands glided down his back, nails raking along his skin all the way to his ass as he pounded her with more fervour. Heat flooded her core, rolling through in waves and, not knowing what to do, she found herself squirming against him, grinding against him, her hips meeting his thrust for thrust. Then, release. Sweet heavenly release!

Her squeals of bliss were masked by his roar. Holding her down, bucking uncontrollably beneath her, he thrust his hips high against hers. She gasped and moaned, the bliss indescribable as she clung to him, clamping her legs ever tighter around him as stars burst around them.

Then, overcome by the scent of her, the thrumming of her blood beneath her skin, he bit her. With a moan he drank deep, suckling the underside of her breast. Her heart pounded wildly against her chest as sweet warmth flooded his mouth. She cried out his name, the bliss overwhelming as he sucked her. When he drew away, blood painted his lips. His eyes were glazed over with euphoria. Kissing her deeply, she could taste the copper tones of her blood upon his tongue and moaned.

"You're so perfect! So damned perfect!" he panted, breath hot against her ears as he held her down in his lap.

And still he came. She could feel his cock buried deep within her, pulsing as warmth flooded out of her, spilling out upon his lap to the grass below.

Then, after a moment of quiet, he kissed her with surprising tenderness, his expression awestruck. "You have undone me," he breathed in sad and wondrous tones. "There is no going back. I am all yours, Lamia."

15

Back to Life

They lay in each other's arms for a good while, laughing and chatting about nothing in particular. Eventually, Lamia began to shiver from the growing cold. Righting her dress, he scooped her up in his arms and carried her from the graveyard, padding across the soft grass.

"Your clothes!"

He smiled lazily, walking through the corridors with her hands wrapped around his shoulders. "There are rumours to uphold."

Laughing as she cast him a disapproving look, he carried her through the endless corridors and down countless steps. She blushed to see Hezron's red cheeks and servants avert their eyes, not to mention the surprised faces of the odd late-night courtier, hoping to wander through the palace undetected. As an embarrassed pair of lovers stopped to bow before the passing Emperor and Queen, Lamia couldn't help but think of the look on Lady Visha's face when she heard the whispered gossip at sunrise.

Shouldering the doors to their private chambers open, Amias pushed the door shut, kissing her hard.

"Now, where were we?" he murmured, approaching the bed.

"You were commenting on how cold I was," she teased, entranced by the glow of his eyes as they grazed over her, finally settling on her lips.

"Oh, yes. And I was gallantly offering to show you some ways to keep you warm," he whispered, depositing her against its cushions and pillows.

"You said you knew *many* ways..." she said, as he crawled over her.

"That I do..." he said, pressing himself hard against her.

"That was quick!" she breathed, heart fluttering to feel him close once more.

"You'll find I'm quite insatiable," he purred, mouth curling into a playful smile. "And I've worked up quite the appetite these past few days... Have I told you how delicious this gown is? I can see *everything...*"

Trailing kisses along their soft curves, he nudged aside her skirts and lifted her legs over his shoulders. Then, gazing down at her, he entered her with delicious ease.

"Exquisite," he groaned, rocking against her in a sublime rhythm. Bracing himself over her, he gripped her tight, tumbling across the sheets. And, entangling their legs and arms around one another, he showed her every wonderful way to keep warm.

Their gasps and moans of delight filled the halls.

SHE AWOKE TO BEING held by him, his hands on her hips, his head nestled against her back. Sunlight filtered through the circular window, but not the weak light of morning. It was at least midday, if not later.

"Oh!" She sat up with a start. "Oh, no!"

Amias looked at her in amusement. He'd propped himself up on one of his elbows, his long hair spilling over his shoulders onto the bed. "Forgotten something?"

She'd reached for the sheets, shyly covering herself. Her sheer gown had been discarded long ago and lay in a heap at the foot of the bed. "I, erh, overslept."

"I'm not surprised. We were *busy* last night." He enunciated carefully, eyes roving over her playfully.

"Why didn't you wake me? Don't you have court?"

He rolled onto his back with a dismissive wave. "I cancelled it. I was too busy enjoying your company to want that of courtiers and barons."

Lamia blushed, though she felt secretly pleased.

"Did you, erh, sleep well?" she asked, for once at a loss for what to say.

"I rarely need sleep, but I enjoyed watching you sleep."

She froze, horrified. "No! You didn't!"

"Oh, I did," he smirked, pulling her to him so she lay atop of him. "I watched you dream, and dreamed of *this*..."

And he kissed her, squeezing her bum cheeks in slow, languid circles.

She hadn't been on top of him before and the change of position was both alluring and unnerving in equal measures. The feel of the taut muscles of his chest below her was massively arousing, and she allowed herself to stroke them. Fingers gliding up and over their sturdy contours.

"Just that?" she teased, aware of him hardening between her legs.

He smiled wolfishly, fangs gleaming. "And *this*."

And, in one swift movement, he slid her down upon him with a groan.

"So soon?" she panted as he filled her.

He smiled to watch the emotions play out on her face as he moved her up and down his hard shaft; the heat rising between them. She found her body moving in time, rocking with increased fervour, all sense leaving her as she braced herself over him, curls cascading in a dark shroud about them as she ground her hips hard against his, meeting him again and again in delightful unison. She was bedevilled. She was possessed. The feeling was indescribable. She couldn't stop herself even if she wanted to; she needed him like a desert needed water. She would take every last bit of him. Everything he offered, and then some.

Rising, nails digging into his shoulders lest the wave of euphoria missed her, her hips slammed hard against his and she cried out in ecstasy as she reached the peak. He held on, hands firm against her hips, his eyes bright with wonder as she threw her head back and cried out.

Dizzy with release, Lamia gasped as he sat upright so they faced one another. His dick still pulsing within her.

Clutching her to him, he kissed her hard. "By the gods! You are so sexy," he growled, pulling away only to kiss her with renewed vigour, lips crashing against hers, tongue prising her mouth open hungrily.

Panting, she gave herself up to him, felt his grip upon her arms as they kissed and kissed, feeling him harden within her to begin again.

A knock at the door caught their attention, and the Emperor eyed Lamia ruefully, gently withdrawing.

"Yes?" he called, wrapping her in the sheets of the bed.

"I have come with food for the Queen, Your Excellency." A muffled voice said through the door.

"Enter."

It was Theodora. Casting Lamia a mischievous grin at their compromising position, she then entered the chamber, directing the two servants that followed her. One set out a meal at the table, whilst the other drew a bath.

"Would that be all, Your Excellency?" Theodora asked, shooing the two servants out with an impatient gesture.

"Yes, thank you, Theodora."

Theodora cast Lamia a last triumphant smirk as she approached the doors.

"There is one last thing," Amias said, taking Lamia's hand in his and raising it to his lips.

"Yes, Your Excellency?" Theodora asked, stopping in surprise.

"Please invite my Queen's parents to a special service of remembrance for their son, Lathan Fontaine, formerly Ward 86789. We shall hold it before dinner in the graveyard. Please notify the High Priest and have him prepare the service."

Lamia searched his eyes in amazement.

He would do this?

For her?

This close, she could see every detail of his purple eyes. They were flecked with gold and glowed like a summer sunset. She felt tears blur her vision.

Theodora curtsied. "Of course, Your Excellency."

"What was your brother's favourite meal?" he asked, squeezing her hand reassuringly.

"Really, you don—"

"What was it?" He repeated with a note of finality. He could not be swayed.

"Venison," she murmured, barely able to speak for the lump in her throat.

"Please have the kitchen prepare venison. My Queen and I shall dine with her family tonight."

"Certainly, Your Excellency."

And Theodora left, bowing deeply.

Lamia stared at him for a long moment. He slowly averted his gaze, a colour washing the pale skin of his cheeks.

"Why would you do that for me?" she stammered, finally finding her voice.

"Just because..." he said, shyly. He smoothed away a tear that had fallen. "Come, let us bathe and eat."

Still clutching the bedsheets to her, Lamia approached the table of food whilst Amias tended to the bath, ensuring it wasn't too hot. The table had been laden with succulent fruits from the palace hot house, as well as wholesome pancakes, yoghurt and homemade chocolates. Suddenly ravenous, she fell on the food, adding berries and a helping honey to the pancakes before devouring two, one after the other.

"My, you are hungry." Amias' voice was behind her, and she hastily finished her mouthful.

"Well, it was an eventful night," she said, feeding some meat to the Felidaeon.

The big cat ate it up and licked its lips. Coming back for more, it nuzzled Lamia's thigh until she fed it another helping. It purred merrily as the girl scratched behind its ears.

"Zora, you traitor!" Amias exclaimed as the Felidaeon rolled over so Lamia could continue fussing it.

Zora looked at Amias with her enormous amber eyes and closed them happily, her purrs rumbling deep in her chest.

He approached to rest on Lamia's shoulder. "Come, the water is perfect."

And he led her to the bathtub with its views of Dårath. Passing a mirror, she glanced at her reflection and was surprised to see her looking better than she had in a long time. The dark shadows that had been there since the knowledge of her brother's illness had lightened.

"Are you alright, My Queen?"

She blushed. "Yes, I... I just wanted to know if I looked different."

He joined her side, though his reflection failed to show in the mirror. "I see the same beautiful woman I saw enter the Chapel. Though you seem lighter. As if a weight has been lifted."

She nodded, absentmindedly touching the curve of her stomach through the sheet. "I feel lighter."

He chuckled, hand covering hers. "You won't be with child just yet."

She glanced up in surprise, her cheeks reddening. "Oh?"

"Only if we..." He hesitated as a redness seem to warm his pale cheeks. "Erh, come *together* during your menses do you come with child. It's your blood, you see. That is why I devised The Picking..."

She blushed. "Oh... Isn't that messy?"

"I like it messy," he purred, his hand guiding hers down between the sheets to touch herself in gentle, delicious, persistent circles.

Arching against his lean body as quivers thrummed through her, she caught sight of her compromising reflection, bright and panting. Though he wasn't visible, it was such a turn on, and she found herself overwhelmed with the heat of a distant promise. She felt him then, lips hot against her ears and jaw, and moaned.

"Go for it, My Queen," he panted into her ear, massaging her into euphoria.

She could feel a swell grow within her, tingling with promise, and threw her head back against his shoulder, hands gripping him for support, holding him close, eyes rolling back in abandon as the waves consumed her.

Sagging against him, relishing the warmth that filled her, he picked her up and carried her to the bath.

"Hopefully, the water is still warm enough," he chuckled.

It was with steam still issuing lazily from the waters. The servant had added a sweet-smelling oil and pale pink petals floated upon its surface.

"This is a tincture that the Palace Thaumaturge formulated from the Elixium Tree. It has great restorative powers and is often used for the Wards to help them relax."

Holding the sheet for her, he watched her step into the bathtub with a contented sigh. As she sploshed in the warm waters, submerging herself for a second, he returned the sheet to the bed before pouring himself some blood from a cooled decanter. He drank heavy and colour flushed his cheeks.

"My, my, you *are* hungry."

He glanced over at her, lips curling into a smile. She was sat soaping herself, petals bobbing around her in tight eddies. Her brow was raised, and a saucy smile pursed her lips.

He strolled over and smiled as her eyes trailed from his face and along his chest to his dick, which hardened with such an audience. She watched him step into the bath, amazed at her lack of shyness—she'd never shared a bath with a man before. Offering his hand, she passed him the sponge, and he pulled her to him, washing her back, trailing the sponge over the wings of her shoulders before rinsing her off. Then, to his surprise, she insisted on doing the same to him, coasting the sponge along the hard contours of his arms and chest under his watchful eye.

Finished, he pulled her close, so she sat between his legs, her back resting lazily against his broad chest. His wet black hair blanketed them. She watched him play with her fingers, intertwining them with his, before trailing his hot fingertips up and down her arms. Lying there, in his arms, the warm waters lapping them, she realised that, for the first time in many months, she was happy. The thought was as surprising as it was unnerving.

Was she supposed to be happy with the man who forced her to marry him?

"I see you asked Theodora to fetch you new roses. They're lovely," he said as his fingers caressed the curve of her inner elbow.

She looked up with a start, eyes finding the vase where she'd left it on the side. The flowers were as red and full as if they had been freshly picked from the palace hot house.

Seeing her shock, he frowned. "They're not new?"

She shook her head. "No, they're the same ones. I-I cut my hand..."

He held up her palm to see the fresh wound upon it. It had healed to a deep pink overnight. He thumbed it tenderly, bringing it to his lips. "Why?"

"To see, to see if it would work again... Like at the chapel..."

He glanced over at the vase of flowers, his eyes keen. "Well, it's safe to say your experiment worked."

DRESSING IN A BLUE velvet gown with the help of Theodora, she met her mother in the gardens, excited to show her the cottage and grounds that the Emperor had gifted her. They had just finished a tour of the gardens with Lamia detailing her plans when her mother squeezed her arm.

"And I gather the Emperor has more planned for us this evening. It is very kind of him to think of Lathan so..."

"It is, isn't it?" Lamia agreed, her cheeks flushing as her thoughts drifted to last night.

A silence followed, and Lamia looked up to find her mother giving her a knowing look.

"You did it, didn't you? Finally!"

"Whatever do you mean?"

"You finally... You know... With the Emperor..."

"Mother!"

"Everyone's talking about it. They say he carried you through the palace naked!" she giggled. A conspiratorial look suddenly appeared in her eyes. "And how was it?"

"Mother!" Lamia felt her cheeks burn.

"I'll take that to mean that it was 'good'. I told you!" She gave her a playful nudge.

At that moment, some gardeners pushing a wheelbarrow of tools appeared. They bowed on seeing Lamia with her mother. "Apologies, Your Majesty! We can come back later."

"No, there's no need," Lamia said.

"Where would you like us to begin, Your Majesty? The Emperor explained how this was to become your garden and sent us to start clearing the borders for you."

Lamia blushed to think of Amias' consideration. "Thank you, that's very kind of you. If you could begin clearing the side borders, I intend to merge the central borders to create a wild meadow."

"That sounds an excellent idea, Your Majesty. Will you be needing a path created?"

"Yes, please. Have you anything I could use to mark it out for you?"

"We have some watered-down paint in the shed?" One of the gardeners said, gesturing to the small wooden structure in the corner.

"Perfect!"

"You and Lathan always enjoyed playing in the meadow back at home," her mother said with a wistful smile.

They watched one of the gardeners fetch a pot of watered-down paint as the other began work on clearing the side borders.

"That's what inspired me. I thought to recreate a bit of home here, for us." She reached for her mother's hand and gave it a squeeze.

"That would be lovely."

WITH THE SUN SETTING, Lamia and her mother went their separate ways to prepare for the service of remembrance for Lathan. Lamia was wandering the corridors, trying to remember her way, when a hand grabbed her from behind, pulling her wrist hard.

"You must be careful, Your Majesty," Lady Visha crooned. "The palace can be a *dangerous* place..." She pointed to the puddle of blood on the tiles. "You wouldn't want to slip and break that pretty little neck of yours."

Lamia glanced from the puddle to the woman with her perfect hair and makeup.

"No, thank you. I'll be more careful from now."

"Please do, the Emperor would miss you terribly. As would I," Lady Visha said with an extravagant curtsy.

Lamia curtsied back and watched the woman glide down the corridor, sidestepping the blood with ease. She glanced down at her wrist where four red blotches remained from where Lady Visha had held her—a sense of unease settling upon her like a cold blanket. Hailing a passing servant, she asked for the blood to be safely cleaned up before hastening to her bedchamber.

THE SERVICE OF REMEMBRANCE was a heartfelt affair. The High Priest must have spoken to her parents as the graveside service contained many anecdotes and happy memories of Lathan that brought a tear to everyone's eye. Even though it was a service for her brother, a lit candle had been placed before all the gravestones so that the woodland shone like a thousand galaxies. Amias looked regal in a black doublet that matched the silk of her gown, black breeches, and leather boots. Not to mention devastatingly gorgeous. She blushed to think that just last night, they'd consummated their marriage on this very spot.

Though I am not seeking a love match...

She found his words ever present in her mind as the hours went on and glanced up to find his eyes on her, hot and brilliant in the candlelight. Blushing deeper, she turned her gaze back to the High Priest, trying to focus on his words.

With a final prayer, the High Priest made a sign of the circle and the Emperor took her mother's hand in his and led her out. Taking her father's proffered hand, they followed them through the graveyard and out into the corridors to a private Dining Room where a grand dinner had been prepared for them.

"He is a good match."

Lamia looked up from her daydream to find her father eyeing her with a warm smile.

"I'm sorry, father."

"Though we wouldn't have thought it, he is a good match for you. You look happier than you have in months."

"Oh, I don't know," she said, brushing aside his compliment. "He is a vampire."

"Has he sucked you dry yet?"

Lamia blushed, thinking of how he had sucked her. "No."

"Then that should not be your measure of him. That is his nature, but not *him*."

Lamia hesitated. "And you don't blame him for Lathan's death?"

Her father looked at her in astonishment. "Of course not! Lathan was ill, very ill and, whilst he fought so hard, it was too much for him," he sniffed, and quickly pulled himself together. "It would have been too much for anyone. And... the Emperor tried, you know. He and his Healers tried so hard to find a cure for him..."

"I-I know..." She looked down at her feet, watching them move in time with her father's.

"So, no, no one is to blame for his death, but death itself."

Lamia pondered this whilst watching Amias walk with her mother, smiling at her as she laughed at some comment he'd made.

"He would want you to be happy, to live and to love, you know," her father continued. "Lathan wouldn't want you to stop enjoying life."

She nodded, "you're right, father." And she marvelled at the warmth that suddenly blossomed within her.

It was only later, when Amias pushed her against their chamber door, hand around her neck as he thumbed her pulse, fangs trailing the curve of her throat, that she realised what the sensation meant.

She gasped as realisation struck, and he chuckled to feel her tense against him, increasing the pleasure as he thrusted, pinning her in place with his hands.

"Is that good? Is that how you like it?"

She nodded, tears pricking her eyes, trying to focus on the feel of him within her and not the pain clutching her heart.

You fool! You damned fool! How could you fall in love when he isn't looking for it?

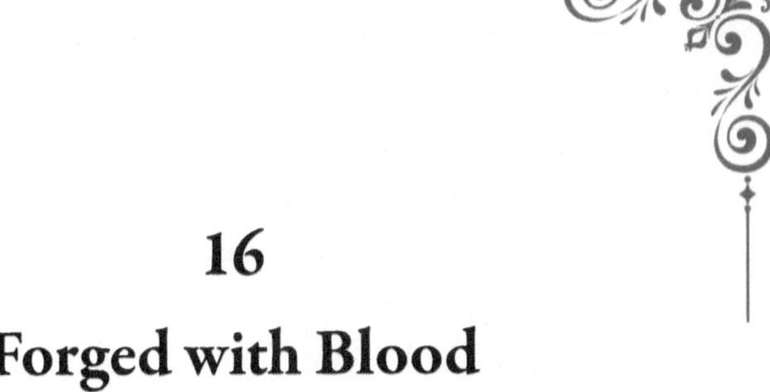

16

Forged with Blood

Weeks passed, and Lamia found herself adjusting to her new life at the palace. Amias had appointed her Ward Carer and put her in charge of the Hospital Wing and the welfare of its Wards and Healers. When she wasn't helping in the Hospital Wing, she busied herself with her garden. Having discovered the magic contained within her blood, she had taken to sneaking a drop or two to the water that she used. So much so that her garden was soon flourishing with flowers and herbs.

One afternoon in late summer, when dressed in work breeches and a shirt, Lamia and a servant were preparing cut flowers for the Hospital Wing—she liked to replenish those in the hospital whilst she made her daily rounds. She'd grown fond of her time chatting to the Wards and the extra responsibility given her. She liked to think of someone being present for her brother in his final days and hoped to do the same for those seeking treatment now. Although only very few Wards grew well enough to leave, and she had had to bid many Wards farewell, she was glad to help in whatever way she could.

"Ward 875453 will love these." The servant said, carefully placing a bunch of flowers in her basket.

"Yes, yellow are Isolabella's favourite." Lamia said, standing to survey the garden, a hand on a hip. The gardeners had worked hard to get the borders just right for her. The wild meadow that had grown created a gentle reminder of those that she and her brother used to play in as children back in Gerran.

It may not have been the future she'd envisioned, but it was all starting to come together beautifully.

Zora head-butted her thigh, nuzzling her before sitting beside her. Lamia reached to scratch behind the Felidaeon's ears just as she liked and smiled to hear her deep purrs.

"Will that be all, Your Majesty?"

"Hmm?" Lamia said distractedly, tearing her gaze from the garden. The sun was setting, casting long shadows across the flowers and shrubs. "Yes, I just need to get some supplies for the Healers. I promised I would. You go on ahead to the Hospital Wing and I'll meet you there."

The servant gave a well-balanced curtsy, being careful not to upset her basket, before leaving the garden for the palace.

"Allow me to come with you," Hezron said from where he stood guard.

Lamia shook her head. "I'll be fine with Zora. If you see the Emperor, please let him know where I am. Come on, Zora," Lamia said, bending to fuss the Felidaeon. "Let's go!"

Together they left the garden at a jog, turning left through the woodland toward the temple of the Elixium Tree. Zora trotted beside her, nipping at a grasshopper. Out of all three Felidaeon, Zora had taken a shine to her and insisted on following her wherever she went, much to Amias' amusement.

After being put in charge of the Hospital Wing, she frequently volunteered to gather fresh supplies of Elixium flowers for the Healers. It saved the Healers' time, and she enjoyed seeing the tree. The sight of it on its island in the middle of the lake, bathed in light, never ceased to take her breath away. There was something holy about it that made her think that, if something so wondrous could exist, then perhaps the gods had once walked these lands after all.

From a distance, it looked as if the tree rested on an island of dirt, but in fact, much of the island was made up of its own roots, with only patches of moss and lawn cushioning its base. At some point in its long life, several smaller branches had been broken off. One portion was virtually dead and had sustained substantial damage with a large branch having been sawn off. Learning this, she had tried to heal it, mixing several drops of her blood with water, but, though it had worked wonders on her garden, it had done nothing for the tree.

Fetching out a small sickle from her belt, she gathered a palmful of flowers to an accompanying prayer.

"What is it, girl?" she said, startled to hear a growl rumble from Zora.

Before she could turn around, there was a hard *thunk!* and she cried out as something sharp embedded itself between her shoulder blades. The pain was hot and deep, burrowing within her with such ferocity it felt like she was being split in two. Vision blurring, she tried to reach behind to whatever was in her back. Fingers brushed against something wooden... *An arrow?*

A lady's scream rang out behind her amidst snarls and growls, and then she heard him roar her name, furious and scared all at once.

"Lamia!"

Amias?

"Amias!" she gasped, confused by the weakness of her voice.

Stumbling as she turned, she caught her foot on a root and fell; the impact pushing the arrow through her ribs with a sickening crack. She gaped to see the metal arrowhead protruding through the gory hole, blood gushing from it in waves. Placing a shaky hand to the wound, it came back soaked with red.

The air fizzled and, looking up, she found her vision ablaze with a bright pink glow from the foliage above, like it was coming to life.

Was it growing?!

Shielding her eyes, she tried to sit upright, but her arms wouldn't work properly. They felt sluggish and seemed unable to support her weight. Gasping for breath as she rolled on to her side, she whimpered to see blood dripping from her lips. Hearing voices, she looked over to the shore to see Amias crouched over a woman's crumpled body, eyes blazing red. He was covered in blood and tearing at the woman's neck. Ripping apart her throat, he drank heavily.

"Amias!" she cried.

His head jerked up and, seeing her alive, his eyes immediately changed back to purple. Tossing the woman's body aside, he leapt over the steppingstones, pouncing with such strength and speed that he became a blur.

"Lamia!"

He was above her, eyes frantic. She felt his touch like a distant memory. She tried to call out his name, but the darkness beckoned, dragging her down into its icy depths...

SHE DIDN'T KNOW HOW much time passed, but she was aware of the darkness fading. A light of appeared at the edges. It was so white and so pure. It grew in strength to banish the darkness and its cold shadows. Then it enveloped her. She knew she ought to be scared, but she wasn't. Its rose-tinted glow warmed her, soothing the aches and pains from her chest and body. Its warmth welcomed her and consoled her, and its power healed her. The light surrounded her in its glory, filling her from within, banishing the eternal darkness that had threatened her.

Eyes snapping open, she spluttered as water suddenly hit her lungs. Panic-stricken, she broke the surface of a pool, gasping for breath. Reaching out with her flailing hands, she found herself cradled in someone's embrace. Water was all around her.

Teeth chattering, she blinked to find herself in the pool of the Elixium Tree.

"Lamia? Lamia?!"

Amias...

Looking up, she found him in the water with her, cradling her fast against him as the icy waters lapped at them. She was covered in thousands of pink petals. An arrow floated nearby.

She smiled weakly up at him, heart warming to see the concern and pain etched upon his face. But, before she could say anything, his mouth found hers as he scattered the lightest of kisses across her lips, cheeks, eyes and brow.

"You're alive?" he choked in amazement.

She nodded, head spinning. Then, his fingers wrapped themselves around her neck, drawing her upwards so their lips met. He kissed her tenderly at first, thumbs caressing her as he drew her closer still, kisses suddenly desperate, tongue worshipping her as it found hers. She kissed him back with just as much fervour, holding on to him as the horror of what had happened caught up on her.

He tasted of blood.

And she loved it.

His hands checked her for injuries, touching and testing, squeezing every last inch of her. Besides the cold and some bruises, the only pain was from her chest where the remains of a nasty gouge could still be seen through her shirt. His fingertips finally came to a stop over the wound. It would scar, but she would live. Resting his forehead against hers, she felt water droplets splosh down on her.

With a start, she looked to see him crying.

"Amias?" Reaching, she wiped his tears from his cheek.

"I thought I'd lost you..." he sobbed, voice raw with emotion. Purple eyes bright with new awareness. "I've only just found you and I thought I'd lost you."

She gaped in astonishment.

"I wanted to surprise you at the cottage. When you weren't there, I remembered you said you were to collect flowers for the Healers. That was when I found her..."

Lamia glanced over at the dead body on the bank now laying in a pool of blood. A crossbow lay nearby. It was Lady Visha. Zora was crouching nearby, tongue lapping at her blood.

Lamis shuddered on seeing the crossbow, loaded with another arrow.

Pulling her closer, the movement tossed the petals upon the surface of the water where they bobbed frantically in tight eddies.

"I didn't know what to do," he admitted, beside himself. "So, I added the flower, as many as I could."

Remembering the glow, Lamia craned her neck to see the tree, eyes widening to see it resplendent and glowing brighter than she'd ever seen.

"Wh-what happened?!"

"I think your blood healed it," he said, carrying her over to it. "All its scars are gone."

With his help, she pulled herself up onto its island to find the spot where she'd fallen covered in her blood. And sparkling. The sparkles glowed through the tree's veins all the way to the portion that had been damaged. Here the glow intensified until the branches themselves seemed to be made of the light. New branches. Branches that hadn't been there before. Pink blossom shimmered from them, lush and luminous. They reached up to the tree's crown, swaying on the breeze.

"It grew back?!" she gasped in astonishment, touching the bark in awe. Suddenly overcome, she pressed her forehead against the tree, biting back tears. "Thank you..."

After several moments, she felt hands on her shoulders, turning her round so her back was pressed against the trunk of the tree.

She stared at him. He looked a mess, worse than she'd ever seen him. Wet and dishevelled, gaunt and paler than usual, his eyes were desperately trained on her as if she might disappear at any minute. She watched breathlessly as he let a hand trail along the line of her chin, stopping close to her lips.

Eyes meeting hers, he smiled. "We should get you out of those wet clothes before you catch a cold."

Allowing herself to be guided away, remembering the petals needed for the Healers, she stumbled past the dead body of Lady Visha and up the steps to the surface. Zora followed beside her. Despite her best efforts, her knees soon gave way and Amias insisted on carrying her.

"Thank you," she said.

"What for?" His gaze seemed rough, his emotions laid bare and, amongst the relief, there was something more...

"For saving me."

He came to an abrupt stop. They were in the forest. She could spy the cottage just through the tree line. Shivering as the early evening breeze mussed her wet hair, she winced against the pain in her chest. As if sensing her discomfort, he shifted her to a more comfortable position.

"Why shouldn't I?" he demanded. He sounded shocked, his voice clipped and high.

She looked away, embarrassed. "Well, I have tried to kill you. Multiple times."

"Who's counting?" he said, lips quirking into a half-smile. He continued walking, carrying her gently but firmly towards the cottage. Smoke rose in purple plumes from its chimney—he must have asked servants to prepare it for them. "Admittedly, my other wives were more compliant, but..." he looked away, eyes suddenly bright. "When I saw the arrow in you, something inside me snapped. I just needed her dead and you alive. And, I realised something else... That I couldn't be without you. That doing so would kill me."

"You can't die," she teased.

"You know what I mean."

Something about the rough tone of his voice made her heart quiver. "I... do?"

Eyes meeting hers, she stared in astonishment at the adoration she saw there. The care, the anguish, and the love...

He rushed on, the colour high in his cheeks. "I know I said this wouldn't be a love match. That I didn't expect it to be a love match, but..." His voice caught in his throat and Lamia found herself clutching at his ruined tunic.

"What? But *what?*" she pleaded, heart hammering frantically against her chest.

They had stopped in the flower gardens she'd created at the front of the cottage, its small wooden door just feet away. He was worrying his lips, she realised, hesitant to continue. He cleared his throat. "I love you. I loved you from the start. I realise that now. After my first wife passed, I promised myself no more. I couldn't stand the grief. But, there is no going back. I cannot help myself... I am destined to love you, destined to long for you, to miss you, and to grieve you."

Blood pounding in her eyes, she was thankful he held her because she didn't think her legs would have been able to keep her from falling.

"You love me?" She repeated dully, hardly daring to believe.

He gripped her tight to him so she faced him, fitting her against him perfectly. "With all my heart. I love you, Lamia Fontaine. All that I am, I give to you. All that I have is yours."

His lips found hers once more, and she sighed against him, heart singing at his words.

He loved her!

She pulled away. "I have a confession."

He looked down at her, eyes filled with devotion, a soft smile on his lips. "And what's that, My Queen?"

He was backing up against the door, which swung open with ease to reveal the living room with a vase of freshly cut flowers and a roaring fire in the hearth.

"Oh!" she gasped, taking in the scene. After the cold of the pool, the warmth of the fire was welcome.

"I said I wanted to surprise you. Now, to get you out of those wet clothes," he said, depositing her on a chair in front of the fire.

She extended her hands out to the fire, relishing its warmth as Amias went upstairs to fetch towels for themselves. Despite her protest, he insisted on unbuttoning her shirt and removing it for her.

"Have I told you how sexy you are dressed like this?" he said, untying her breeches.

She laughed as he dried her. "Only every time I wear them!"

"Especially when you have no undergarments on." He pulled her to him, inhaling against the feel of her breasts pushed up against him. He shoved his hands down the waistband of her breeches so they cuffed her bum cheeks. "You said you had a confession?"

She nodded, heart suddenly pounding against her ribs. He regarded her carefully, head canted as if he could hear it.

"Yes, I..." Her throat was suddenly dry.

Pressing a hand against her chest, he caught her eye. "Your heart... Is everything alright?"

She stammered, the breath catching in her throat as she prepared to tell him. "I... I love you too."

He stared at her, eyes widening in shock. "You do?"

"I've loved you for a while now." She rushed on lest her courage failed her. "I knew you said you didn't want a love match, so I didn't sa—"

He silenced her with a kiss so fierce it took her breath away. She was glad when his arms appeared around her because her knees felt like they might give way from under her.

"I can be such a damned fool!" he cursed, pulling away to press his forehead against hers. "Can you forgive me?"

"Always."

He thumbed her cheeks, and he kissed her again, drawing her ever closer to explore her, hands roaming along her naked back and hips. His touch sparked against her skin, setting her core on fire. Then, a smile tugging his lips, he pulled her into the simple kitchen, its table laid out with dinner for her.

"So, you love me and I love you?"

His hands pushed her breeches down further, revealing her. Her heart fluttered as she felt his arousal rear up.

"So it would appear, My Queen. And you're naked. And I'm *almost* naked."

Swiping the kitchen table clear, sending its contents crashing to the floor, he lifted her onto the wooden surface. Peeling off her breeches, massaging her thighs and calves as he went, he then whipped them off, flinging them out of the way.

"How very astute of you, My Lord."

He looked up at her sultry tones, eyes alight with hunger.

"It would be rude not to," she added, smiling coyly, spreading her legs wide so he could see her in her full glory.

He groaned as she began to touch herself. "Temptress!"

Scrambling out of his jerkin and breeches, she inhaled as his dick and balls spilled out, hard and ready. He approached, eyes set on hers, their glow intense.

"And we wouldn't want to waste this," she murmured, cupping his bulging manhood with both hands.

He gasped, eyes rolling back as she caressed him. A growl rumbled at the back of his throat, and he grabbed her hands, clamping them against the tabletop. Then, with one sharp thrust, he slid his cock home.

She gasped against the bliss.

"You're so damned perfect!" he sighed, mouth covering hers, tongue exploring every inch, whipping her into a frenzy as he kissed her again and again.

Sucking his lower lip, she wrapped both legs around his waist and drew him further in.

"By the Gods!" he swore.

"I'm going to make you scream my name."

He looked up to see the wanton gleam in her eyes and chuckled. "I'd gladly scream your name all day and all night, My Queen."

She wrapped her arms around his neck, head thrown back, legs wide as she ground against him, controlling the depth and her pleasure. And he pounded her, grunting like some beast as his hands moved to her ass, clutching her as he thrusted harder and harder, hips meeting hers again and again.

"You're so wet!" he ground out.

"That's all for you," she cried, feeling his dick bucking within her as he came, spilling out of her.

The familiar warmth spread between her legs as she neared climax.

"Don't stop!" she pleaded, feeling the warmth fade as he slowed.

Leaning back, she pushed him further in, grinding against him in desperation.

"Fuck, Lamia!" he cried, as his cock throbbed again and again, spilling more of his seed.

It hit her then, the purest of euphoria and she let out a cry of ecstasy, nails raking his shoulders as she rode it.

Spent, she sagged against him, moaning to feel kisses scatter across her shoulders and collarbone. Leaning back, she kissed him hard.

"I love you," he said, resting his forehead against hers and sighed a happy sigh.

"And I love you," she said, smiling back.

As he removed his shaft from her, he looked down in surprise. "Since when did you start your menses?"

Epilogue

A year later

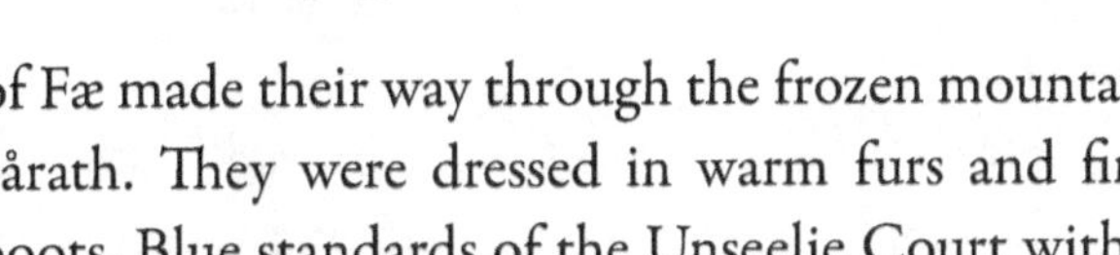

The entourage of Fæ made their way through the frozen mountain passes near Dårath. They were dressed in warm furs and fine leather jerkins and boots. Blue standards of the Unseelie Court with a moon embroidered in silver glittered in the late summer breeze. As always, this high up, the air was biting. But, to make matters worse, the section of road they were on was in the shade.

A young male Fæ rode towards the front alongside another, hood pulled up against the chill. A long white braid plaited with a leather cord drooped down his shoulder.

"How much farther?" moaned his Fæ companion, who had brown hair and a matching brown tail with a tuft of hair at its tip.

"Not long. If I remember correctly, it's just after that bend," he said, pointing to the approaching corner.

His companion sighed and burrowed himself further down into his saddle. He pulled his fur-lined hood up closer against the cold, his tail swishing irritably.

"I hope it reveals the sun. I could do with its warmth on my back, not all of us are blessed with Winter's Kiss!" he grumbled.

His friend chuckled, turning his steely blue eyes to him, their white snowflake patterns stark. Before he could say anything, a sharp voice called them from behind.

"I hope you two aren't up to more mischief!"

Stopping their horses, they turned to find a tall and imposing man approach upon a great white stallion. A helmet with fashioned antlers bearing a crown was upon his head.

"Of course not, Your Majesty," the brown-haired man said, colour rising in his cheeks.

"Oh, I'm not so worried about you, Lord Roan," said King Morozko of the Winter Court. "I'm more concerned about Prince Boreas. You're nothing compared to him."

Roan didn't know whether to look relieved or aggrieved.

Boreas patted him on the back. "I would take that as a compliment."

"He should," said Morozko, cutting Boreas a look.

They rode on in silence, rounding the curve to reveal a sweeping landscape of glaciers, ravines and snowy peaks. In the distance was a walled city. A towering palace scratched the heavens: Dårath, Noxterra's capital.

"At last!" sighed Roan.

"It certainly is a welcome sight!" King Morozko admitted. "It has been a long road."

"It's hard to believe it's only been a year since we were last here!" Boreas said, spurring his mount on—another white stallion which had a black half star on its face.

"Your great-great-uncle doesn't waste any time!"

Boreas flashed Roan a knowing look.

"I'm looking forward to seeing my new niece. If your aunt is anything to go by, she'll be a beauty," the King said, continuing. "Talking of which, I think it's high time we looked at a wife for you, Boreas."

The Prince stopped short, pulling on his horses' reins. "But, father, I've still yet to finish my training at Nathair Caisteal!"

The King waved aside his protest. "You are entering your third and final year of training in Draakonia. Once you graduate as a dragon rider, you will have proven yourself worthy to succeed as Captain of the Keep at the Unseelie Court. You will also be eighty and ready to settle down."

"He's the same age as me and not yet wed!" Boreas declared, pointing at Roan, who was flashing him a cocky smile.

"Lord Roan isn't tasked with securing an heir to the Winter Court."

"I'm not either! That's Aquilo's job!"

"There's always room for a spare."

Boreas rolled his eyes. His father really was no fun—it was all about duty with him.

"I should be honoured to assist the Prince, Your Majesty. Might I suggest Lord Wright's daughter? She would make a fine match."

King Morozko looked thoughtful. "Not a bad idea, Roan! I'll mention it to Hendrick."

Boreas cut him a look. Lord Wright's daughter was renowned for having bad breath and bad wind.

Roan smiled smugly as he bowed to the King who pulled back to talk with his Right Hand, Hendrick.

"What in the name of *all* the Gods are you playing at?!" Boreas hissed.

"Just looking out for you, dear friend," he said, still looking smug. You'd make the worst of matches on your own." Roan urged his mount forward and they canted away.

Boreas watched him go with baleful eyes, sorrow gripping his heart.

THE VISITORS WERE WARMLY welcomed into Dårath with much merriment and cheers as they made their way along Dårath Boulevard to the Eternal Palace. The Emperor had given the capital a week's holiday to celebrate the safe arrival of his first child with Queen Lamia of Gerran.

Passing through the gates, they were met in person by Emperor Amias. He was dressed all in blue and looked the happiest Boreas had ever seen him.

"Morozko! I'm so glad to see you well! Thank you so much for making such an effort to attend the princess' Naming Day," he said, embracing his relative once the King had dismounted.

"We wouldn't have missed it for the world, Your Excellency!" Morozko said, returning the embrace. "Prince Aquilo sends his apologies. I have left him in command in my absence."

"A baptism of fire!" The Emperor chuckled.

"Quite possibly."

Rûntal stepped forward to embrace Boreas. "Welcome, cousin. Let us get you settled into your quarters before you meet with the Queen."

Shown to their quarters, Boreas was relieved to see him sharing with Roan—there was never a dull moment with him nearby. Bathing, they changed into jerkins with the Winter Court's moon emblem emblazoned on its breast and prepared to meet the Queen.

"Maybe you could find someone in the Emperor's court?" Roan suggested, eyeing up a couple of ladies as they made their way to the celebrations.

Boreas glanced over his shoulder at the retreating ladies. "You know I prefer curves."

"I know, I know. And I'm seeing *plenty* of curves!"

"You seek a bride then."

"Not until I've assisted you, dear friend."

"How very bloody kind of you..." Boreas sighed.

Roan looked up in surprise. "Whatever's the matter? I was only joking about Lord Wright's daughter."

"I know..."

"So, what is it?"

The doors of the court were before them, open to reveal the revelry within.

Boreas suddenly looked embarrassed and adjusted his jerkin. "It's nothing."

"The hell it is—you're never this serious. Out with it!"

Boreas stopped short when Roan's hand appeared on him. But, before he could reply, the Herald announced their arrival to the court.

"Prince Boreas de Marc and Lord Roan of Loxwood!"

The effect was immediate, and within seconds, they were surrounded by women dressed in their finest silks. Roan was beside himself, quickly selecting a lady for each arm and smiling wolfishly at Boreas, his tail twitching. At least someone loved the 'prince effect'...

"Boreas!"

Turning, he found himself before his father and his great-uncle. Quickly regaining his composure, he bowed before finding his great-uncle's arm about his shoulder.

"Your father was telling me about you entering the final year of your training at Nathair Caisteal! He says you're going to be promoted to Squadron Leader!" Amias said, looking at him with pride. "Congratulations! I know the training is tough, but our family has attended for centuries. I know you shan't let the Court down."

"Thank you, great-uncle."

"What are your plans now?"

His father stepped forward. "Once he graduates, he shall be appointed Captain of the Keep as he fulfils his duty to his brother and the Court. There is also the matter of a wife..."

"About time!" Amias squeezed his shoulders reassuringly as the colour left Boreas' face. The young Fæ grinned nervously at his great-uncle. Amias turned to Morozko. "Has a match been made for Aquilo?"

At that moment, Lamia appeared, carrying a small bundle wrapped in a delicately crocheted blanket.

The men immediately bowed low, except Amias, who beamed, pulling her close.

"My Queen! How I've missed you," he kissed her cheek, putting an arm around her before admiring their daughter with an indulgent smile. "How is she?"

"Well, she threw up all over Vasilis."

Amias burst out laughing. *"Ha!* I'm sorry to have missed that!"

"His face was quite the picture! Elyssia was beside herself," Lamia replied with a barely suppressed grin.

"You remember my great-nephew King Morozko and his youngest son Prince Boreas?" Amias said.

"Of course! Thank you so much for journeying to celebrate the princess' Naming Day tomorrow," said Lamia.

"The pleasure is all ours, Your Majesty." Morozko observed the baby girl. "As I thought," he said in matter-of-fact tones, "she's as beautiful as her mother."

Lamia laughed shyly. "You're too kind, Your Majesty!"

"It is the truth, though."

Indeed, it was. The princess was beautiful, with ochre skin, a headful of curls, chubby cheeks, long lashes and violet eyes. Though her fangs had yet to grow through, the pointed tips of her ears could just be seen amidst her curly locks.

"She is perfect, isn't she?" Lamia sighed, gazing from her daughter to Amias with dreamy eyes.

Amias smiled back. "She is."

Boreas looked at the scene before him and swallowed awkwardly. It felt far too private.

Excusing himself, Boreas took a turn of the room, greeting people and ensuring he'd been seen before selecting a flute of champagne and slipping out onto the terrace which overlooked the palace gardens. Since The Picking, when the new queen had been found, the gardens had been transformed and were even more resplendent than they had been before. Stopping to lean against the balustrades, he looked out over the moonlit bathed grounds with a sigh.

There is also the matter of a wife...

"You seemed a little pensive, Boreas. I was worried."

Boreas turned to find Lamia standing close by, her daughter cradled in her arms.

Quickly standing to attention, Boreas bowed. "Your Majesty!"

Lamia gave a dismissive snort. "Please, Boreas, we're family. Call me, 'Lamia.'"

He bowed more deeply, cheeks reddening. "I love the gardens. You've truly transformed them, Lamia."

"Thank you. It's certainly a passion of mine."

Boreas took a sip of his champagne and looked out over the landscaped grounds with another sigh.

"Talking of passion, what are you really doing out here, Boreas?"

The Prince looked up with heavy eyes before glancing quickly away.

"I know we've only met a few times, but I feel quite a kinship with you. I hope I can be a confidant for you."

"You're too kind, Your Majesty."

"'Lamia.'" She corrected. She looked at the young Fæ Prince before her with his white hair, chiselled lines, and startling snowflake patterned eyes. His brow was low, and shadows blackened his gaze. "Might I hazard a guess?"

"Of course," he said, an amused twinkle appearing in his eyes.

Lamia considered him for a moment. "Well, you strike me as too easygoing to be concerned about your promotion to Squadron Leader, nor your graduation next year. I think it has more to do with your father's eagerness for you to marry."

Boreas looked down at his feet. "I'm sorry to be so easily read."

She touched his shoulder reassuringly. "Hardly. I'm just well-versed in matters of the heart."

There was a companionable silence as they looked out across the gardens.

"It's a wondrous thing, being in love," she continued. "Admittedly, the Emperor and I had our differences at the start of our relationship."

A ghost of a smile appeared on Boreas's lips. *That was an understatement!*

"But I'm sure you will fare better than us," she smiled reassuringly.

He suddenly looked stricken with pain, and tears washed his eyes. He turned away to brace himself against the balustrade, head bowed. "I don't think so... The lady I love doesn't love me. I've... I've already asked..."

Lamia looked at him, heartbroken. "Oh, I'm so sorry!"

"Thank you, but I am doomed to a life of misery."

She placed a hand on his shoulder. "Oh, come now, Boreas! Don't be like that. Perhaps she just needs time to assess her feelings."

"She needs no time." He looked away bitterly.

"Would you like me to speak to her on your behalf? I can be quite persuasive."

"I do not doubt! But, alas..." He shook his head. "Her mind is made up. There is nothing anybody can do."

"And might I ask who this girl who broke your heart is?"

"Rosaline Fairbrair, a fellow student at Nathair Caisteal."

To be continued in *Of Wings & Fury*
Warring Hearts 2

Of Wings & Fury

Fourth Wing* meets *Romeo and Juliet*. This fantasy romance
retelling about a Fæ Prince from the Winter Court and his
forbidden romance with the Fæ Princess of the Summer Court is
impossible to put down!*

Prince Boreas is eager to start his last year at Nathair Caisteal, the
famous dragon rider school of Draakonia. Anything to heal his broken
heart. But when Princess Idalia of the Summer Court enters her first
year, sparks fly. And not just from their dragons. He tells himself it's
because of their family's history, nothing more, nothing less.

Princess Idalia is finally living her dream as a trainee dragon rider
at Nathair Caisteal. Though the course is demanding and the constant
threat of 'death by dragon' lingers in the air. Turns out Boreas, the son
of her family's rivals, is also a student there. It isn't before long attempts
on her life begin. Despite being her prime suspect, Idalia is surprised to
learn Boreas isn't behind the attacks. She's even more surprised to find
him determined to help her survive till graduation. Is it purely to keep
his family's name in the clear, or does he have an ulterior motive? Or is
that just wishful thinking on her part?

*Of Wings & Fury is a complete *standalone, enemies-to-lovers
novella* inspired by the ultimate star-crossed lovers, Romeo and
Juliet. With magic, spice and a <u>guaranteed</u> happily ever after—it's
perfect for fantasy romance fans looking for their next hot read!*
Coming December 2024

Available for pre-order here: https://books2read.com/ofwingsandfury
*[Sign up to my Romantasy Books mailing list to be the first to see the cover and learn about ARC opportunities: **https://beacons.ai/ georgianakentbooks**]*

Acknowledgements

***

The biggest 'thank you' goes to my Alpha Readers, Bethan and Krista Walsh, for taking the time to read my first draft and provide feedback. You're awesome and amazing and I can't thank you enough for your help, especially when I know how busy you both are. It was an honour working with you! A special thank you to my FAKA author friends for all your support this past year—knowing you has made this author journey far less lonely. I'm so blessed to have you in my life. A big 'thank you' to everyone on TikTok for your support of this book. I'm so excited to see where we go next. Thank you to my editor for your help, support and suggestions—sorry it was so rushed in the end! Thank you to Tania and the team at GetCovers for creating such a gorgeous cover! You captured all the feels of *Of Blood & Roses* perfectly! Thank you to my family for your unending support and confidence in me and my writing. A special thank you to my darling hubby. Thank you for your support with my writing. It means the world to me. And thank you for the inspiration! There's always a little of you in each of my bad boys.

About the Author

***

Join Georgiana's *Romantasy Books* mailing list to stay updated on giveaways, releases, sales, and more. Sign up here: https://beacons.ai/georgianakentbooks

Georgiana Kent has always been creative and loves telling stories of fantasy worlds filled with magic, mystery and more. Her books are fantasies on an epic scale with unique world-building, and a host of strong, diverse characters waiting for you to fall in love with. For fans of contemporary fantasies featuring mystery, shifters, time travel, and slow-burn romance, the *Soul Dominion* series is a must-read. When she's not writing, you can find her enjoying time with her family in the Peak District. She and her family share their home with their rescue kitten, affectionately known as 'Panda Cat', who rules them all.

Find Me Here

***

Social platforms, playlists and other cool stuff: https://beacons.ai/
georgianakentbooks

My website:
https://bit.ly/GeorgianaKentHome

Find me on Facebook, Instagram and TikTok!
@authorgeorgianakent @romantasybooks

If you would like to leave a review, you can do so here:
https://books2read.com/ofbloodandroses/
Hashtags:
#georgianakent #warringhearts #myrrithia

www.ingramcontent.com/pod-product-compliance
Lightning Source LLC
Chambersburg PA
CBHW031551150726
47990CB00001B/307